Norroway

Book 2: The Queen on the High Mountain

Words by Cat Seaton
Pictures by Kit Seaton

Editorial by Shanna Matuszak
Design by Deanna Phelps
Proofing by Melissa Gifford

SIBYLLA TIBBON

Following a prophecy she was told as a child, Sibylla left Goose Valley at age seventeen to marry the Black Bull of Norroway and break his curse.

PETRA

Sibylla's faithful magpie companion.

BROM HAUGEN

A former prince of Norroway, Brom is cursed to roam the countryside as a monstrous bull as payment for his family's sins.

ESBEN HAUGEN

Another exiled prince, Brom's inventor brother Esben now lives in an accursed castle with a loyal entourage of two: George, the knight, and Mathilde, his scullery maid.

MAIRE SYLVANA

A forest witch known as the Old One, Maire foretold Sibylla's future as a child, only to later reveal she was the one who cursed Norroway in the first place.

DAGNY HAUGEN

Brom's sister Dagny murdered her husband, a member of the Troll Kingdom's royal family, then fled Norroway with her lover, Captain Harper Dhow.

CAPTAIN HARPER DHOW

Harper Dhow, Dagny's lover and the former captain of the Fleetfoot, flew into a rage and sunk their ship in an attempt to kill Brom.

ONCE UPON A TIME...

Three sisters went deep into the woods searching for the forest witch, hoping the gifts they carried would be payment enough for a glimpse at their futures. There, the littlest sister learned of the grievous prophecy that would shape her destiny. She would marry a wicked knight, the Black Bull of Norroway, and break a curse that crippled the land.

Years later, that foretold knight arrived for the girl in the form of a giant bull. They crossed the Narrow Sea and climbed the Glass Mountain, and the girl learned the truth about the knight's curse. The king, the knight's father, had ordered him to sacrifice one of his sisters to the Old One in exchange for power. Enraged by the king's despicable command and the loathsome knight's obedience, the Old One instead cursed them all: the king, the knight, and the entire Kingdom of Norroway.

Horrified by the knight's actions and his refusal to answer any questions, the girl wanted to give up. Instead, she decided to seize her fate and help the knight defeat the Old One.

After reaching the battlefield, only one rule was given: do not interfere. However, the knight had gone unarmed into the fray, and the girl knew he would surely die without her help, so she defied the Old One and bravely brought him his sword.

She interfered, and the battle was lost.

Her attempt to help the great bull knight failed and sent her tumbling down the Glass Mountain into the harbor town of Fiskeby, separating them...but not for long...

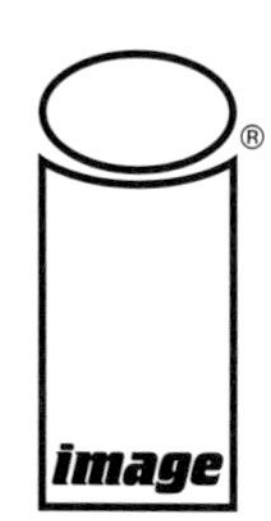

NORROWAY, BOOK 2: THE QUEEN ON THE HIGH MOUNTAIN. First printing. April 2021. Published by Image Comics, Inc. Office of publication: PO BOX 14457, Portland, OR 97293. Printed in the USA. For international rights, contact: foreignlicensing@imagecomics.com. ISBN: 978-1-5343-1607-2.

FISKEBY.

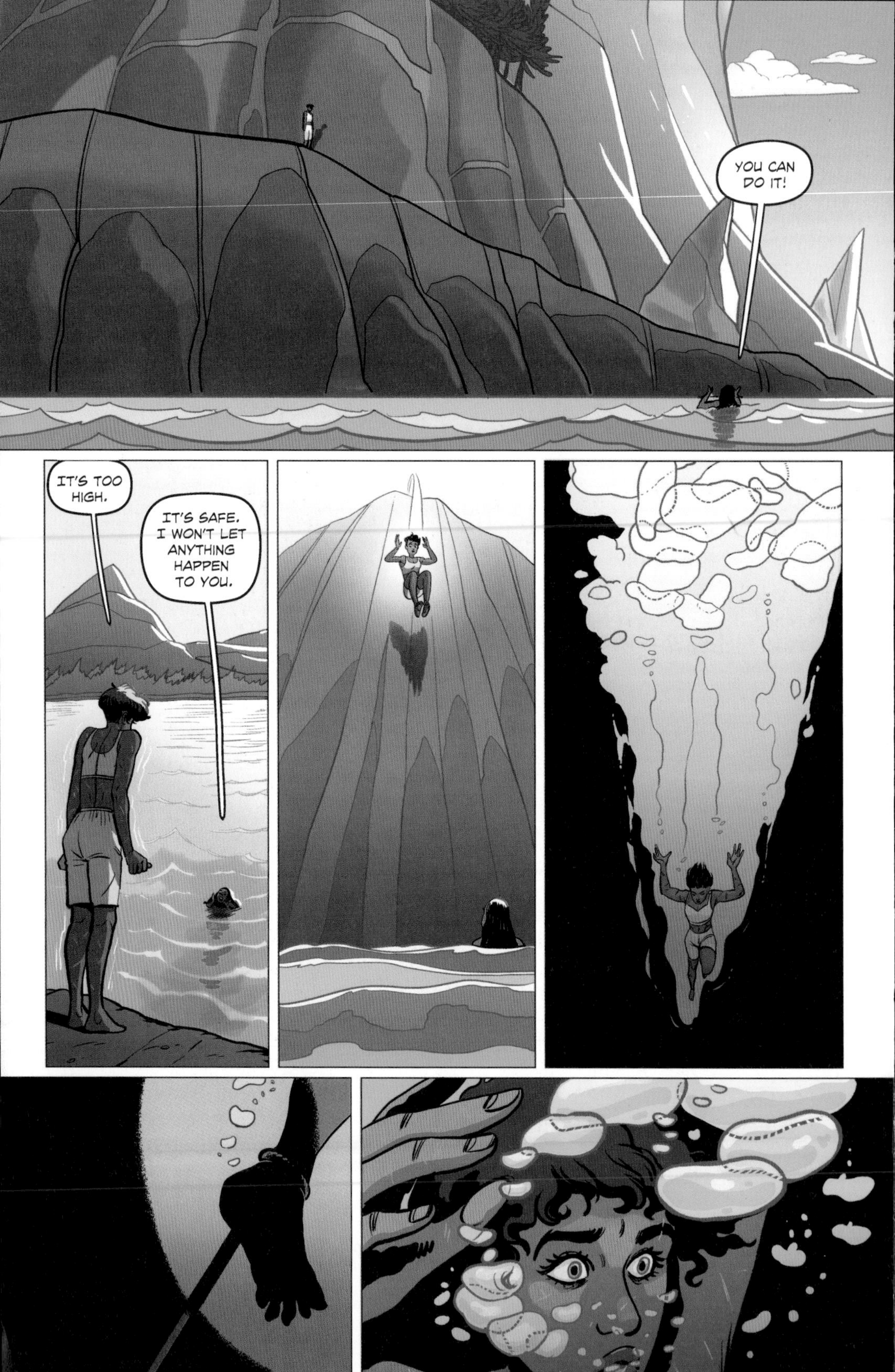

YOU CAN DO IT!
IT'S TOO HIGH.
IT'S SAFE. I WON'T LET ANYTHING HAPPEN TO YOU.

EASY! YOU'RE ALL RIGHT! EVERYTHING'S ALL RIGHT.
I'M SORRY.
GILLS, SIBYLLA. THERE'S NOTHING TO BE SORRY ABOUT.
I MADE THE JUMP JUST FINE LAST TIME...
I THOUGHT—
THESE THINGS TAKE TIME.
IT'S BEEN SO LONG, GILLY!
AND I CAN'T EVEN— I CAN'T—
IT'S LIKE A SPLINTER THAT'S TOO DEEP TO GET OUT, BUT IT NEVER STOPS HURTING.
SOME FOLKS NEVER GET BACK IN THE WATER AFTER A SHIPWRECK. YOU'RE MAKING PROGRESS.
REMEMBER WHEN YOU PUNCHED MY DAD FOR TRYING TO PUSH YOU OFF THE DOCK?
YEAH.
SEE? PROGRESS.
LET'S GET DRESSED, THEN YOU CAN TEACH ME THE *WORD* FOR *FIRE*.

ffff
Pff

FWOOOSH

CLAP-CLAP-CLAP!

DO YOU WANT TO HEAR A STORY?
IS IT ANOTHER SEA STORY?
...NO.
NO? IT WASN'T A STORY ABOUT A MAN WHO CATCHES A MAGIC FISH AND SPARES ITS LIFE FOR WISHES?
OR A WOMAN WRAPPED IN NETS, HALF RIDING A DONKEY, WHO OUTSMARTS A KING?
BOTH OF THOSE ARE VERY GOOD STORIES.
WE'LL MAKE A BETTER ONE.
FULL OF ADVENTURE AND, DARE I SAY, ROMANCE?
WHAT ELSE WOULD IT BE FULL OF?
STALLING, APPARENTLY. I STILL SAY DAD WOULD HAVE LET YOU OUT OF THE APPRENTICESHIP MONTHS AGO.
YES, BUT... I PROMISED YOUR FATHER SEVEN YEARS, AND I HAVE THE SHOES TO FINISH AND–
IT'S ALWAYS SOMETHING, ISN'T IT?
WE'LL GO, GILLY. I'M JUST NOT READY YET. SOON.
...DO YOU WANT TO LEARN ANOTHER *WORD?*

WHICH ONE?

NORROWAY

THE QUEEN ON THE HIGH MOUNTAIN

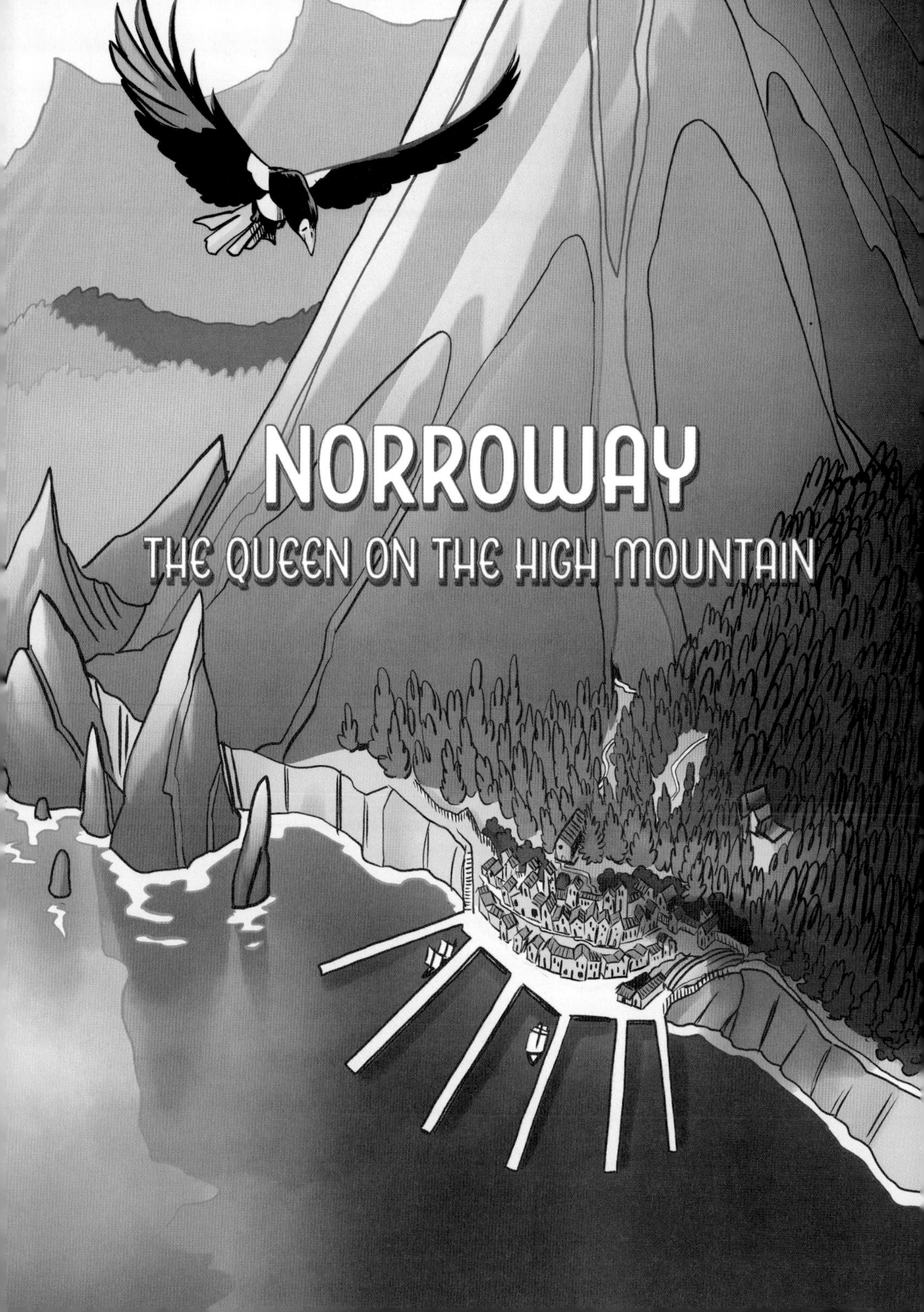

SIX MONTHS LATER...
AN ENTIRE FIN! FOR POTATOES?! NEXT THING YOU KNOW THEY'LL BE ASKING ME TO PAY A WHOLE FISH!
CAN YOU BELIEVE THE NERVE OF–
AND WHERE ARE YOU OFF TO IN SUCH A HURRY?

GOOD TIDES, EDIE. FLO. I'M RUNNING A LITTLE LATE FOR LUNCH.
SAFE HARBORS TO YOU. HOW'S YOUR FATHER?
WELL ENOUGH. THE TROLLS ARE KEEPING THE SMITHY BUSY.
IT'S NOT A BAD THING TO HAVE A BIT OF HONEST WORK.
HONEST, IS IT?! WITH PRICES THE WAY THEY ARE SINCE THEY SCARED OFF ALL THE TRADE-
SSSHHH...
TCH.
DO YOU HAVE ANY BAGUETTES LEFT?
I'M AFRAID I'VE SOLD THE LAST ONE.
YOU KNOW YOU HAVE TO COME EARLIER.
IT'S ALL RIGHT. I'LL TAKE A FEW OF THE JAMMY GUPPIES THEN.
YOU'RE COMING TO DINNER TONIGHT, AREN'T YOU?
INVITE SIBYLLA AND YOUR FATHER- I KNOW IT'S A HARD DAY OF THE YEAR FOR HIM.
AND FOR YOU.
THE FOXBERRY CORDIAL'S FINALLY READY TO DRINK.
NOT EVEN THE DOLDRUMS COULD STOP US. FAIR WINDS!

RADHA. GOOD MORNING.
WITH THE SUN SO HIGH IN THE SKY?
YOU WERE OUT WITH THE SEALS AGAIN THIS MORNING, WEREN'T YOU?
THEY'VE GOT A LOT OF STORIES TO TELL ABOUT MOM.
OF COURSE. I HAVE SOMEONE HERE WHO WANTS TO MEET YOU.
THIS IS BEATRICE DHOW.
BEA, THIS IS GILLIAN GUMBOULT, EDUN'S DAUGHTER.
A PLEASURE TO MEET YOU.
I SEE SO FEW SEAL-FOLK THESE DAYS.
I SEE YOU GOT THE LAST BAGUETTE. ARE YOU NEW HERE?
I'VE BEEN HERE A FEW DAYS SELLING MY ORANGES.
NOW *THOSE* ARE A THING OF BEAUTY.
HOW-
I CAN'T SAY HOW THEY-OR I MYSELF, FOR THAT MATTER-GOT HERE, BUT I'D BE HAPPY TO TRADE YOU FOR SOME.
I'VE GOT THREE SCALES, A FIN, AND TWO TAILS.
WHAT'S AN OLD WOMAN TO DO WITH MONEY?
I'LL TAKE A BIT OF INFORMATION INSTEAD.

WHAT DO YOU WANT TO KNOW?
I'VE HEARD YOU KNOW A BIT OF SPEAKING.
IS THAT TRUE?
GILLS, WHO TOLD YOU THAT?
USING THE WORDS IS A RARE SKILL, AND A USEFUL ONE. PEOPLE TALK.
I'LL LOOK FOR PEOPLE WITH ORANGES THEN...
LOOK, I ONLY KNOW A COUPLE, AND I'M NOT MUCH GOOD AT THEM IF THAT'S WHAT YOU'RE WONDERING.
COULD I HEAR THEM?
WHAT?! HERE?!
ARE YOU COMPLETELY CAPSIZED?!
NOT HERE. YOU'LL HAVE TO FORGIVE AN OLD WOMAN.
THE SOUND OF THEM MAKES ME NOSTALGIC.
MY TWIN COULD USE THEM, AND...
IT'S HARD TO LET GO OF A MEMORY, YOU MUST KNOW THAT.
NO, I...
WAS THAT ALL YOU WANTED TO KNOW?
JUST ONE MORE QUESTION.
WHAT WAS IT LIKE BEFORE THE TROLLS CAME?

WELL, THE MARKET WAS FULL OF PEOPLE FROM ALL OVER THE KINGDOM.
MY MOTHER COULD GET HER MEDICINE, AND WE DIDN'T HAVE TO WORRY ABOUT FOOD OR HOW MUCH IT COST.
MY FATHER MADE GATES AND HORSESHOES INSTEAD OF SWORDS AND SHIELDS.
IF THAT'S ALL, I'VE GOT TO GET GOING. BUSY, YOU KNOW. NO TIME TO DWELL ON THE PAST.
THANK YOU FOR THE ORANGES. FAIR WINDS, RADHA. BEATRICE.

SIBYLLA!

SWEATY.
SORRY.

I HAVE QUITE THE SURPRISE FOR YOU.
OH?
IN MY INFINITE GREATNESS, I HAVE ACQUIRED A RARE DELICACY.
OH INDEED! ORANGES, IF YOU CAN BELIEVE IT!
THE OLD WOMAN I GOT THEM FROM WAS A BIT OVERBOARD, YOU KNOW, BUT–
HOLD ON. WHAT'S THAT?
WHAT'S WHAT?

ANOTHER PAIR?! REALLY?!
NOTHING'S BEEN QUITE RIGHT YET.

BUT THEY'RE NEVER GOING TO ***BE*** QUITE RIGHT, ARE THEY?
YOUR APPRENTICESHIP ENDED! AND YOU ***SAID*** "AT THE END OF SEVEN YEARS"–
THAT WAS ONLY A FEW DAYS AGO.

BUT YOU QUIT YOUR JOB AT THE APOTHECARY, WEEKS AGO.
I THOUGHT WE WOULD BE GONE BY NOW.
I JUST NEED THE SHOES TO BE RIGHT.
ONCE I HAVE THEM FIGURED OUT, IT WON'T TAKE ANY TIME TO MAKE US BOTH A PAIR, I PROMISE.
I'M NOT GOING TO LET YOU OFF THE HOOK FOREVER.
YOU SHOULD KEEP ME ON THE HOOK.
I'M REALLY QUITE A GOOD CATCH.
DEBATABLE. I THINK I OUGHT TO THROW YOU BACK.
BUT A FISH OF MY CALIBER–
YOU'RE NOT A FISH AT ALL, YOU'RE A HERMIT CRAB. HOLED UP HERE, OR IN FLO'S APOTHECARY ALL DAY.
WELL, A *CRAB* OF MY CALIBER–
THESE LOOK FINE. JUST...
FORGET IT. WHERE'S DAD?
HE'S GOING TO SETTLE UP WITH THE TROLLS.
A SHIP COMES IN TODAY AND HE DOESN'T WANT ANYONE TO SKIP TOWN.
OH. EVEN MORE TROLLS COMING DOWN FROM THEIR GLASS KINGDOM.
I WISH THEY'D STAY THERE.
MM.

SURE WOULD BE NICE IF WE LEFT BEFORE THEY TOOK OVER THE WHOLE TOWN...
MMHMM.
JUST CLIMB UP THE GLASS MOUNTAIN WITH MY GIRLFRIEND, LIKE SHE PROMISED...
YOU DO REALIZE THAT JUST GETS US CLOSER TO THE TROLLS, DON'T YOU?
THEN LET'S GO SOMEWHERE ELSE!
WHAT?
THEN YOU WON'T EVEN NEED TO WORRY ABOUT THE SHOES!
WE COULD BUY PASSAGE ABOARD ONE OF THE SHIPS THAT COMES THROUGH–
I KNOW YOU HATE BOATS, BUT YOU'VE BEEN DOING SO WELL LATELY. WE JUST HAVE TO GET OUT OF THIS COVE.
AFTER THAT WE COULD GO ANYWHERE. YOU AND ME.
THERE'S NO NEED TO GO AND FIND BROM, IT'S NOT LIKE YOU'RE GOING TO MARRY HIM ANYWAY.
WELL, NO, BUT THE CURSE–
LISTEN TO ME, THE CURSE IS NOT YOUR RESPONSIBILITY. SEVEN YEARS IS UP, SIBYLLA! AND YOU MADE A PROMISE!
I JUST– I HAVEN'T–
ALL OF MY THINGS ARE HERE.
I'D NEED TO FIGURE OUT WHAT TO DO WITH THEM.
SELL THEM, LEAVE THEM.
THROW THEM INTO THE OCEAN FOR ALL I CARE!
I CAN'T JUST UP AND–
NOT WHILE YOUR DAD IS SO BUSY–

MY DAD SURVIVED WITHOUT AN APPRENTICE FOR YEARS, AND I'M SURE SOMEONE WOULD BE HAPPY TO TAKE YOUR PLACE.
I JUST-
JUST WHAT? DO YOU NOT WANT TO GO? DO YOU WANT TO STAY HERE?
NO! NO, I JUST.
I NEED MORE TIME, GILLY.
I'M NOT READY.
WILL YOU EVER BE READY, SIBS? OR WILL IT BE ANOTHER SEVEN YEARS?
WILL YOU JUST KEEP MELTING SHOE AFTER SHOE, MAKING EXCUSE AFTER EXCUSE?
THAT'S NOT WHAT I'M DOING, GILLY, I'M-
I DON'T WANT TO STAY HERE! FISKEBY IS DYING! I'M TIRED OF SEEING TROLLS EVERY DAY OF MY LIFE! DO YOU HAVE ANY IDEA-
LOOK, I CAN'T WAIT FOREVER. I KNOW IT'S HARD FOR YOU, AND I KNOW THAT MAYBE IT'S NOT FAIR TO ASK BUT...
PLEASE, SIBYLLA. I WANT YOU TO COME WITH ME. I WANT US TO GO TOGETHER. JUST SAY YOU WANT TO GO WITH ME.
PLEASE.
FINE. ***FINE.*** I'M GOING TO GO PICK UP SOME THINGS FROM RADHA.
I EXPECT I'LL LEAVE WITHIN THE WEEK. LET ME KNOW WHAT YOU DECIDE...

IT'S BEEN SEVEN YEARS, PETRA!
I MISSED YOU!
SO THAT'S IT, IS IT? YOU WANT ME TO LEAVE TOO.

NEW FRIEND?
OLD PEST.
HOW ARE YOU, FLORENCE?
JUST ENJOYING THE BREEZE. IT'LL BE COLD SOON, YOU CAN FEEL IT IN THE WIND.
I THOUGHT YOU PREFERRED THE SUMMER?
OH SURE, BUT THE COLD'S GOOD FOR BUSINESS.
LOTS OF WINTER SNIFFLES.
I CAN'T TELL IF YOU'RE BEING SERIOUS.
NO, NO. OF COURSE NOT.

THAT ONE'S LIT UP LIKE A FESTIVAL, DON'T YOU THINK?
MM.
I'M GUESSING THERE'S SOMETHING ON YOUR MIND?
NO... YES.
GILLY'S LEAVING.
WHAT?
I DON'T KNOW WHEN, BUT SOON. SHE WANTS TO GO, AND I WANT TO STAY.
AT LEAST I THINK I WANT TO STAY, BUT NOW PETRA'S BACK–
THAT'S PETRA?
AYE. THAT'S HER. SHE WANTS ME TO CLIMB THE GLASS MOUNTAIN, BUT FOR WHAT?
SOME WITCH'S CURSE FROM WHEN I WAS A LITTLE GIRL. I DON'T CARE ANYMORE! NOT ABOUT MAGIC OR TROLLS OR MAKING SHOES.
I JUST– I DON'T KNOW WHAT TO DO. I DON'T WANT GILLY TO LEAVE.
IT SEEMED TO ME LIKE YOU PLANNED TO GO. YOU QUIT THE SHOP WEEKS AGO.

I KNOW. I DID WANT TO GO, BUT NOW I JUST DON'T KNOW.
I FEEL LIKE I'M FALLING.
I WANT TO BE HAPPY HERE, BUT IF GILLY LEAVES—
I JUST FEEL LIKE NOTHING I SAY OR DO MATTERS.
I NEVER REALLY MAKE MY OWN CHOICES.
SHARING A LIFE WITH SOMEONE MEANS SHARING OUR CHOICES, AND OUR CONSEQUENCES.
I KNOW YOU AND GILLY. YOU'LL CATCH EACH OTHER.
IT'LL WORK OUT.
BELIEVE ME, I'VE SURVIVED A FEW TUMBLES MYSELF.
NOW THEN, THAT SHIP LOOKED IMPORTANT, DIDN'T IT?
OH, FLO. IT SEEMS LIKE NO MATTER HOW HIGH I CLIMB, I FEEL SO TRAPPED.
I'M GOING TO GO TRADE THESE TINCTURES FOR SOME ORANGES DOWN BY THE DOCKS.
WHY NOT COME WITH ME AND SEE WHAT ALL THE FUSS IS ABOUT?

CAPTAIN TEMUR.
WHAT BRINGS YOU TO OUR SHORES?
WHY, EDITH FISK, I DO BELIEVE YOU ARE TRYING TO MAKE ME FEEL UNWELCOME.
NO, NO. OF COURSE NOT. I ONLY—WE DIDN'T—IT'S JUST THAT WE DIDN'T KNOW YOU WERE COMING, AND SOMEONE OF YOUR POSITION, IT—
MY MOVEMENTS ARE MY OWN TO TEND TO, AND IT WOULD DO YOU WELL TO REMEMBER THAT.
OF COURSE.
YES. THIS WILL DO.
CAPTAIN?

CALL A COUNCIL MEETING FOR THIS EVENING AT SUNDOWN, EDNA.
I'VE ORDERS FROM THE QUEEN TO DISCUSS WITH YOU.
I-IT'S EDITH-
I KNOW.
YOU THERE.
ME?
YOU'RE THE APOTHECARY, ARE YOU NOT?
YOU WILL TAKE THIS SMALL RETINUE AND MYSELF ON A BRIEF TOUR OF THE VILLAGE AND THE SURROUNDING FLORA.
I SHOULD LIKE TO KNOW ALL ITS LITTLE NOOKS AND CRANNIES.
SHE'S VERY BUSY, CAPTAIN, WHAT WITH COLD SEASON AND-
IT'S FINE, EDIE.
FOLLOW ME.

MISS GUMBOULT!
BEA.
WHAT DO YOU MAKE OF ALL THIS?
NOTHING GOOD.
NO DOUBT THE TROLLS ARE HERE TO IMPOSE MORE SANCTIONS.
THAT'S WHY I WANTED TO TELL YOU...
I CAME TO FISKEBY FROM ACROSS THE NARROW SEA, AFTER THE TROLLS DESTROYED MY VILLAGE.
THEY ATTACKED YOU?
DIDN'T NEED TO. WE DIDN'T GIVE THEM OUR SUPPORT, SO THEY CUT US OFF.
OUR TOWN SURVIVED ON SALT AND GOODS BROUGHT IN FROM NORROWAY. WHEN THE TRADE DRIED UP...
WE LEFT, OR WE STARVED.
THAT'S BLEAK.
OUR TOWN WON'T BE THE ONLY ONE TO SUFFER.
THE TROLLS ARE JUST GOING TO KEEP SPREADING, AREN'T THEY?
AYE. THAT IS THE WAY OF KINGDOMS.

BUT NORROWAY RULED BEFORE–
AND NORROWAY WAS RULED BY A MAD KING.
THE CURSE THAT TRAPPED HIM BENEATH THE GLASS WAS A BLESSING FOR US LITTLE FOLK.
PEOPLE WILL ALWAYS SUFFER UNDER THE RULE OF KINGS.
I DON'T REALLY SEE A WAY AROUND IT.
THERE ARE WAYS TO TOPPLE KINGDOMS.
YOU WON'T FIND SUPPORT FOR THOSE SORTS OF IDEAS HERE.
OUR TOWN IS...FINE.
IT'S GOING TO BE FINE. I...
GOOD TIDES, BEA. I'LL SEE YOU LATER.

THAT EVENING...
WHAT A LOVELY TOWN YOU HAVE. IT'S A SHAME I'VE NEVER EXPLORED IT BEFORE TODAY.
THANK YOU...
I WANTED TO BE CERTAIN OUR QUEEN HAD MADE THE RIGHT DECISION, AND NOW THAT I'VE SEEN IT FOR MYSELF, I MUST SAY I WAS A FOOL TO DOUBT HER.
WHAT AN HONOR IT WILL BE FOR YOU.
WHAT AN HONOR?
TO BECOME THE COMMERCE CAPITAL OF THE REUNIFIED KINGDOM.
REUNIFIED?

THE LAST LIVING PRINCE OF NORROWAY IS TO MARRY THE QUEEN'S DAUGHTER, BEQUEATHING HIS LANDS TO THE TROLL KINGDOM IN THE PROCESS.
WE ARE MARCHING TOWARDS PEACE, AND YOU ARE FORTUNATE ENOUGH TO WITNESS IT.
MARRYING THE-
AND WHAT OF THE LADY DAGNY?
THAT VILE MURDERESS WILL HAVE HER DUE. AS ANY THREAT TO THE NEW KINGDOM SHOULD EXPECT.
HER INFLUENCE IS BEING EXCISED AS WE SPEAK.
AND THE KING-
DON'T BE SIMPLE. THE KING IS INDISPOSED. HE'LL BE TRAPPED BENEATH THE GLASS FOR ETERNITY EVER AFTER.
NORROWAY IS CRUMBLING- SURELY YOU'VE SEEN HOW YOUR TRADE HAS SUFFERED, HOW YOUR PEOPLE HAVE SUFFERED.
I VISITED FISKEBY DURING MY YOUTH WHEN THE PORT WAS AS BUSTLING AS THE GOBLIN MARKET ITSELF.
YOU WILL HAVE THAT AGAIN UNDER TROLL KINGDOM RULE, YOU NEED ONLY SWEAR YOUR FEALTY TO US.

WHAT NEED HAVE YOU OF OUR FEALTY WHEN YOU'VE ALREADY TAKEN WHAT YOU WANTED? YOUR SOLDIERS HAVE BEEN HERE FOR YEARS!
IT'S THE PRINCIPLE OF THE THING.
IF FISKEBY IS THE FIRST TO RECOGNIZE THE TROLL KINGDOM, YOUR NEIGHBORS WILL NOT BE SO EAGER TO REBEL.
STEP DOWN. ELECT A TROLL COUNCIL. WE WILL FORTIFY THE CITY. WE WILL KEEP YOUR PEOPLE SAFE FROM ANY DANGERS THAT MAY THREATEN YOU.
YOU DON'T WANT A COMMERCE CAPITAL, YOU WANT A MILITARY OUTPOST.
WHY NOT BOTH? FISKEBY SITS AT THE BASE OF THE GLASS.
IT GUARDS ONE OF TWO PORTS TO THE NARROW SEA, AND OF COURSE THE TROLL KINGDOM ITSELF. SURELY YOU CAN SEE WHY THE QUEEN MUST HAVE IT.
AND IF WE SAY NO?
THERE IS NO "NO." YOU SAID YOURSELF WE'VE TAKEN FISKEBY ALREADY.
THE WAY I SEE IT, YOU HAVE TWO OPTIONS.
TAKE THIS RATHER GENEROUS AND PROFITABLE ARRANGEMENT, OR WE WILL FIND A NEW METHOD OF SECURING YOUR AGREEMENT.
WE'RE ALL CREATURES OF LOGIC HERE, ARE WE NOT?
I'M CERTAIN YOU'LL COME TO THE RIGHT DECISION.

YOU HAVE UNTIL TOMORROW AT DAWN.
QUEEN NOG MAY BE PATIENT, BUT I AM NOT.
SO THAT'S IT? YOU'RE JUST GOING TO LET THEM DO IT?
GILLY, WHAT ARE YOU DOING HERE?
YOU TOLD ME TO TRY AND BE MORE INVOLVED IN VILLAGE POLITICS, DAD. WELL, HERE I AM.
THEY'VE ALREADY DONE IT, GILLIAN. OR DIDN'T YOU HEAR?
IT WILL BE ALL RIGHT, DEAR-
NO! IT WON'T!
THERE'S NO REASON TO BE RUDE-
ARE MY MANNERS REALLY GOING TO BE THE FOCUS RIGHT NOW?
LOOK. WE HAVE TO COOPERATE-
WE DON'T!
SHH!

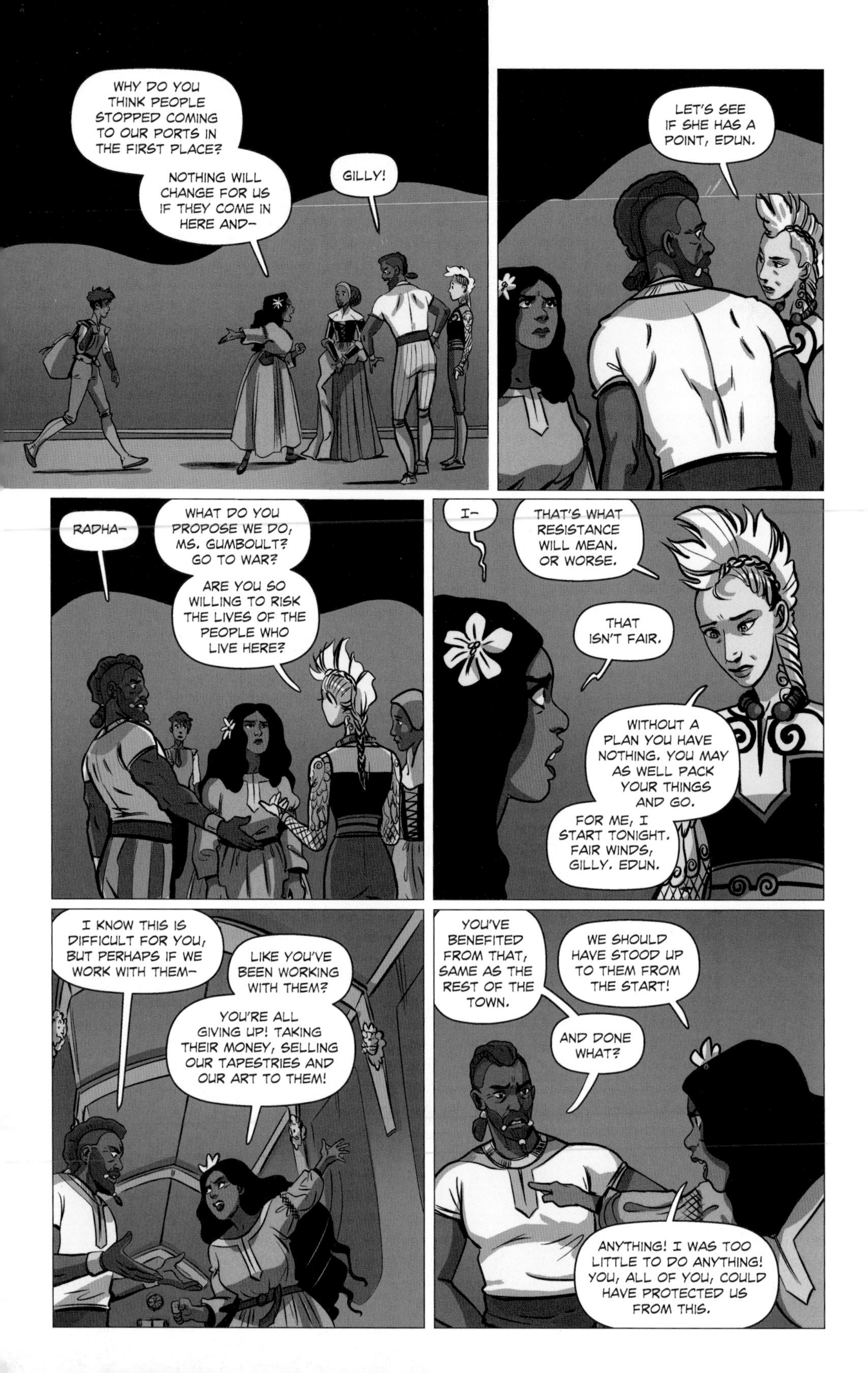

WHY DO YOU THINK PEOPLE STOPPED COMING TO OUR PORTS IN THE FIRST PLACE?
NOTHING WILL CHANGE FOR US IF THEY COME IN HERE AND—
GILLY!
LET'S SEE IF SHE HAS A POINT, EDUN.
RADHA—
WHAT DO YOU PROPOSE WE DO, MS. GUMBOULT? GO TO WAR?
ARE YOU SO WILLING TO RISK THE LIVES OF THE PEOPLE WHO LIVE HERE?
I—
THAT'S WHAT RESISTANCE WILL MEAN. OR WORSE.
THAT ISN'T FAIR.
WITHOUT A PLAN YOU HAVE NOTHING. YOU MAY AS WELL PACK YOUR THINGS AND GO.
FOR ME, I START TONIGHT. FAIR WINDS, GILLY. EDUN.
I KNOW THIS IS DIFFICULT FOR YOU, BUT PERHAPS IF WE WORK WITH THEM—
LIKE YOU'VE BEEN WORKING WITH THEM?
YOU'RE ALL GIVING UP! TAKING THEIR MONEY, SELLING OUR TAPESTRIES AND OUR ART TO THEM!
YOU'VE BENEFITED FROM THAT, SAME AS THE REST OF THE TOWN.
WE SHOULD HAVE STOOD UP TO THEM FROM THE START!
AND DONE WHAT?
ANYTHING! I WAS TOO LITTLE TO DO ANYTHING! YOU, ALL OF YOU, COULD HAVE PROTECTED US FROM THIS.

IT REALLY ISN'T THAT BAD–
BECAUSE YOU'RE SO CAUGHT UP IN IT YOU CAN'T SEE PAST IT!
GILLIAN. THIS ISN'T A CHOICE. WE'LL BE GIVING FISKEBY TO THE TROLLS.
GILLS TO THAT! THEY KILLED MOM!
YOUR MOTHER DIED BECAUSE SHE WAS SICK.
AND WE COULDN'T GET THE MEDICINE! STAND UP FOR YOURSELF!
GILLY–
I CAN'T BELIEVE–
AND ON TODAY OF ALL DAYS?
I DON'T KNOW HOW MOM EVER COULD HAVE MARRIED A COWARD LIKE YOU.

EDUN, I'M SORRY–
NO, I...
I CAN GO TALK TO HER? SHE CAN'T HAVE MEANT WHAT SHE SAID.
I'M NOT SO SURE ABOUT THAT.
IT'S THE ANNIVERSARY OF BRONAGH'S DEATH. THE GIRL SIMPLY MISSES HER MOTHER.
I THINK IT'S GONE WELL BEYOND SORROW.
I'LL GO.
WAIT! GILLY!
I HATE THIS! I HATE THEM!
I KNOW.
AND NOW– WE CAN'T–
THERE'S NOTHING WE CAN–!
NOW, DEAR. I WOULDN'T GET SO UPSET. THERE'S OTHER WAYS TO FIGHT THESE THINGS THAN HEAD ON. WILL YOU COME ON A WALK WITH ME?
FINE.
COME ALONG.

RADHA.
YOU KNOW I CAME FROM HONEYBORN, DON'T YOU? SAME AS BEA.
I DIDN'T, NO.
IT WAS A GOOD TOWN. I HAD HOPED TO GO BACK TO IT EVENTUALLY.
A GHOST TOWN NOW.
WAS THAT THE TROLLS TOO? THEY CLAIM THEY'RE GOING TO HELP FISKEBY–
BUT THEY WON'T.
MAYBE AT FIRST. BUT BEFORE LONG THE TROLL KINGDOM WILL BE DOING AS IT PLEASES.
AND THEN IT WILL BE FAR TOO LATE TO SAY A WORD AGAINST IT. YOU'LL SEE.
THEN LET'S FIND A WAY TO BREAK THE CURSE AND LET NORROWAY DEAL WITH THEM.
ABSOLUTELY NOT. NO KINGDOM IS KIND, AND YOU NEED TO UNDERSTAND THAT.
BUT IT COULDN'T HAVE BEEN AS BAD AS–
THEY TOOK MY TWIN FROM ME.

NORROWAY LOVED A PRETTY CHILD. WE WERE ONLY SIX YEARS OLD. LOST IN THE WOODS FOR HOURS.
SOMETIME BEFORE WE FOUND OUR WAY OUT, WE WERE SEPARATED.
I STILL DON'T KNOW HOW, AND AFTER ALL THESE YEARS MAYBE IT DOESN'T MATTER.
BUT WHAT I FOUND IN THE WOODS THAT DAY WASN'T MY TWIN. THEY'D LEFT A CHANGELING IN HARPER'S PLACE.
AN UGLY, BLOTCHY-FACED, GANGLY CUCKOO.
MY MOTHER NURTURED THAT HOWLING THING FOR YEARS; IT WAS THE WEIGHT OF IT THAT KILLED HER. AND SHE WASN'T THE FIRST. SHE WASN'T THE LAST.
I'M SORRY.

YOU THINK I'M HERE FOR YOUR PITY? BE ANGRY. KNOW WHAT THE LAST KINGDOM DID TO US, AND THAT THE TROLL KINGDOM WILL FOLLOW IN THEIR FOOTSTEPS.
WHAT GOOD DOES ANGER DO ME?
I THOUGHT YOU SAID YOU WERE PACKING.
I SAID I STARTED TONIGHT—
I DIDN'T SAY I'D BE PACKING.
SO WHAT'S THE PLAN?
NO TROLLS, NO NORROWAY. WE WANT OUR OWN RULES AND OUR OWN RULERS.
ALL TEN OF US.
THERE ARE MANY MORE ALL OVER THE COUNTRY. THEY'LL COME IF WE SHOW THEM WE'RE WILLING TO FIGHT.
WHAT WOULD WE BE DOING?

CAPTAIN MAL TEMUR IS THE QUEEN'S RIGHT HAND, WE'LL TAKE CARE OF HER FIRST. WE'LL STEAL THE BOATS, WE'LL HARRY THEM, WE'LL SET FIRES—
WE'LL COMMIT MURDER—?
IF THE TASK CALLS FOR IT.
GILLY! I'M SO GLAD I— OH.
CONGRATULATIONS, YOU FOUND ME.
WHAT'S GOING ON? WHO IS THIS? WAIT. I COULD SWEAR I'VE SEEN YOU BEFORE.
REUNIONS LATER.
WHY DID YOU FOLLOW ME?
A LONG TIME AGO ON THE OTHER SIDE OF THE NARROW SEA. I WAS FATTER THEN.
YOU SEEMED UPSET.
OBVIOUSLY I'M UPSET, OR WERE YOU NOT PAYING ATTENTION? THE COUNCIL'S GONE CAPSIZED, AND WE'LL ALL DROWN WITH THEM.
I DON'T THINK THAT'S—

DON'T TELL ME YOU'RE WITH *THEM.*
THE COUNCIL DOESN'T WANT ANYONE TO GET HURT.
PEOPLE ARE ALREADY HURTING! BEA LOST HER VILLAGE! MY MOTHER IS DEAD!
AND THE FOOD WE HAVE IN OUR VILLAGE IS LITTLE BETTER THAN SCRAPS– BECAUSE OF THEM!
AND WHO KNOWS HOW MANY OTHER THINGS THEY'VE DONE, HOW MANY OTHER LIVES THEY'VE RUINED?
OH, BUT THAT'S ALL GOING TO BE OK, ISN'T IT? WE'LL BE SAFE! THE PRINCE AND THE PRINCESS WILL BE MARRIED!
CALM DOWN–
DON'T TELL ME TO BE CALM! WHY AREN'T YOU ANGRY? DO YOU THINK THEY'LL KEEP ANY OF THEIR PROMISES?
I DON'T KNOW WHAT YOU THINK WE CAN DO–
I'M FIGHTING BACK. WE ARE. BEA AND RADHA AND ALL OF THEM. WE'RE GOING TO FIGHT THIS.
I DON'T THINK IT NEEDS TO COME TO FIGHTING–
GILLS, SIBYLLA! ARE YOU KIDDING ME? DON'T YOU STAND UP FOR ANYTHING?
A FEW HOURS AGO YOU WANTED TO LEAVE!
NOW SUDDENLY YOU WANT TO STAY AND–WHAT? START A REBELLION?
I DON'T KNOW WHAT YOU WANT FROM ME!

I WANT YOU TO CARE ENOUGH ABOUT SOMETHING THAT YOU'LL ACTUALLY MAKE AN EFFORT!
I WANT YOU TO STOP THINKING THAT IF YOU IGNORE SOMETHING LONG ENOUGH, IT'LL JUST GO AWAY!
THINGS ARE GOING TO KEEP GETTING WORSE, SIBYLLA. GIVING A DAMN ABOUT SOMETHING IS HOW IT GETS BETTER!
I JUST– I–
WE'RE DONE HERE.
GILLY, PLEASE! JUST! WAIT! I BROUGHT–
I DON'T WANT TO LOSE–
CRASH!
SLAP!

WOOOOSH!!!
SNAP!
THUD

I CAN'T! I CAN'T.
COME ON, GILLY! WE HAVE TO GO!
THEY SAW US, THEY SAW YOU-
I KILLED- SIBYLLA, I- AND-
GILLY, IT WAS AN ACCIDENT. COME ON.

THEY HAVE BEA–
GILLIAN GUMBOULT, YOU LISTEN TO ME. YOU ARE THE STRONGEST PERSON I KNOW, OK? YOU'VE GOT TO KEEP BEING THAT PERSON, AT LEAST FOR NOW.
FOR NOW, YOU'VE GOT TO KEEP GOING.
I DIDN'T MEAN TO DO IT. I DIDN'T WANT–
I KNOW YOU DIDN'T.
I KNOW. BUT WE HAVE TO GO, OK?
WE HAVE TO GO.
SIBYLLA! GILLIAN!
EDUN!
I'M SO GLAD YOU'RE ALL RIGHT. WHEN I COULDN'T FIND YOU–
DAD–
I HEARD WHAT HAPPENED. THAT CAPTAIN TEMUR FOUND RADHA AND THE OTHERS MEETING AT FENN'S GROVE.
THAT A GUARD IS DEAD. THEY'RE ARRESTING EVERYONE, ANYONE THEY THINK IS SUSPICIOUS. I THOUGHT–
THANK THE WINDS YOU'RE ALL RIGHT, I WAS SO WORRIED–
IT WAS ME!

WHAT?
I KILLED THE GUARD.
A TREE BRANCH FELL. IT WAS AN ACCIDENT! SHE DIDN'T MEAN TO! WE WERE THERE WITH THE REST OF THEM—
OH, NO. OH, GILLY.
DAD, I'M SCARED.
YOU'VE GOT TO LEAVE.
BUT—
NO. YOU'RE LEAVING. BOTH OF YOU ARE LEAVING.

I'M SORRY.
YOU'LL BE ALL RIGHT.
WE'LL FIND EACH OTHER AGAIN. I PROMISE. TAKE THIS.
DAD...
GET OUT OF HERE!
COME WITH ME. YOU CAN HOLD ON TO ME, WE'LL—
I CAN'T. YOU KNOW I CAN'T.
THEN WHERE WILL YOU GO?

I FINISHED THEM. I WAS GOING TO TELL YOU.
SIBYLLA...
I LOVE YOU, GILLY.
I LOVE YOU TOO, HERMIT CRAB.
GO. I'LL FIND YOU AS SOON AS I CAN. THE NEXT BEACH OR... OR ANYWHERE. I'LL FIND YOU.
PROMISE?
PROMISE.

WAIT!
GO!

hee
hee
hee
HAHAHAHAHAHAHA
HAAA
Snif-

I GUESS WE'RE DOING THIS, AREN'T WE?

THE TROLL KINGDOM.

FIVE...
SIX...
SEVEN...
EIGHT...
NINE...*TEN!*
READY OR NOT, HERE I COME!

GOT YOU!

MISS LOTA!
I LEAVE TO GO AND FETCH OUR LUNCH, AND LOOK AT THE STATE OF YOU!
MOPP-

NO, NO! NO "MOPP"!
YOU'VE A DRESS FITTING TODAY, AND THE QUEEN WILL BE RIGHT DISAPPOINTED IN ME FOR YOUR... UTTER DISHEVELMENT.
SHE'S ONLY HALF SO BAD AS SHE USUALLY IS.
AND YOU, SIR! DRAGGING OUR SWEET GIRL TO THE WITCH'S WOOD!
STRANGE THINGS HAPPEN SO NEAR THIS STREAM!
WHY, WHEN I WAS A LITTLE HOGLET, BACK WHEN I'D JUST COME TO THE PALACE, THERE WAS THIS STABLE BOY AND HE–
HE STEPPED INTO WHAT LOOKED LIKE SHALLOW WATER AND IT SWALLOWED HIM WITHOUT A TRACE, YES, WE KNOW.
IT WAS ONLY A BIT OF FUN.

FUN? HARDLY! IF THE QUEEN WERE TO FIND OUT–
DO YOU PLAN TO TELL THE QUEEN?
WELL, N–NO–
THEN SHE'LL NOT FIND OUT, WILL SHE?
flump!
SHE FINDS EVERYTHING OUT, SIR! AS YOU WELL SHOULD KNOW!
WE'RE STILL IN SIGHT OF THE GARDENS, YOU SILLY THING.
THIS WON'T HAVE MADE ANY TROUBLE FOR US.
boop!

I'VE GOT IT.
SIR, IT IS MY JOB TO SERVE THE LADY–
HONESTLY, IT'S NO BOTHER TO PICK UP A FEW...
THAT'S QUITE ENOUGH OF THAT, AND I'LL THANK YOU TO HAVE THE GOOD SENSE TO WAIT UP THERE ON THE HILL WITH–

WAIT! SIR! IT MAY BE DANGEROUS!

SHE MAY BE DEAD OR CARRYING SOME SORT OF A PLAGUE, SIR-
SHE'S NOT DEAD, SHE'S BREATH-
MOPP!
POKE!
HU-WHA!
AAAA

GUARDS! GUARDS!
RIGHT. NO ARROWS...

MURDERER! ASSASSIN! GUARDS!
MOPP!

WHERE-

WHO ARE YOU? HOW DID YOU-
I-PLEASE, WAIT! I'M LOST!
BROM, STOP!
BROM-?

I'M JUST TRYING TO FIND MY WAY BACK TO THE NARROW SEA, AND TO GILLY–
THE NARROW SEA IS FAR FROM HERE. WHO ARE YOU?
MY NAME IS SIBYLLA TIBBON. I'VE BEEN LOST IN THE WOODS FOR DAYS. PLEASE...

NO! NO, PLEASE!

BROM! IT'S ME! YOU KNOW ME! TELL THEM!

I DON'T-
SHE'S A
STRANGER.
YOU KNOW
ME! BROM!
BROM!
BROM?
ARE YOU...?

WENT INTO THE WOODS, YOU TWO DID. INVITED THAT ASSASSIN RIGHT IN, THE BOTH OF YOU.
LUCKY I WAS THERE AND ACTED QUICKLY. I SAVED ALL OF OUR LIVES.
OH, MOPP. PLEASE.
BROM?
SORRY, I JUST...
YOU DIDN'T KNOW HER, DID YOU?
I DON'T... THINK...
HAVE YOU REMEMBERED SOMETHING?
SHE SEEMED FAMILIAR SOMEHOW, BUT I COULD BE FOOLING MYSELF.
fwup

IT'S POSSIBLE YOU RECOGNIZED HER AS A DANGER.
SHE WOULDN'T BE THE FIRST TO TRY AND UNDERMINE THE WEDDING, THOUGH SHE'S THE FIRST TO GO AFTER YOU OR THE PRINCE, MISS LOTA.
SHE CAME FROM SO NEAR THE WITCH'S WOOD, THAT'S TROUBLING...
I SUPPOSE WE'LL NEED TO INCREASE THE GUARDS-
LOTA?
I WOULD LIKE TO SPEAK WITH HER.
MY MOTHER WOULD NEVER ALLOW IT. SHE'S CLEARLY A CRIMINAL-
WE DON'T EVEN KNOW WHY SHE'S HERE.
AND IT MIGHT UPSET YOUR CONDITION.
OF COURSE IT MIGHT.
EVERYTHING SEEMS TO, DOESN'T IT?
YOU'RE GETTING BETTER, LOVE. THE FITS ARE COMING LESS FREQUENTLY.
AND PERHAPS, AFTER THE STRESS OF THE WEDDING-
PERHAPS.

I'LL BE GLAD WHEN THIS BUSINESS IS OVER AND DONE WITH.
ARE YOU CERTAIN IT'S WHAT YOU WANT, LOTA?
WHY? AREN'T YOU?
IT'S FOR THE GOOD OF THE KINGDOM. THAT'S WHAT YOUR MOTHER KEEPS TELLING US.
SHE THINKS IT WILL STOP MOST OF THE FIGHTING... AND BESIDES-

DON'T UPSET YOURSELF...
WOULD IT PLEASE YOU IF I SPOKE TO MOTHER ABOUT THE GIRL?
YOU WOULD DO THAT?
IT DOES NOT TROUBLE ME TO DO SO SMALL A THING.
THANK YOU, LOTA.
YOU ARE TOO GOOD TO ME.
I AM. STAY HERE, I'LL FETCH A GUARD TO HELP YOU TEND TO YOUR HEADACHE.
huffle

THAT WAS PARTICULARLY UNINTELLIGENT OF YOU.

EXCUSE ME-
CAPTAIN DHOW!?
FANCY MEETING YOU HERE, SIBYLLA.
HOW-
TROLLS.
YOU KNOW, I FIGURED AS MUCH.
I WASN'T SURE YOU WOULD.
...THEY BURNED DOWN THE PALACE.
THEY WHAT? DAGNY'S PALACE!? WHY!?

THE TROLL QUEEN'S BROTHER. HE WAS DAGNY'S HUSBAND.
THE ONE SHE-?
DID THEY CATCH HER TOO? IS SHE GOING TO BE ALL RIGHT?
WHAT KIND OF A QUESTION IS THAT?!
THEY BURNED DOWN THE PALACE! IT'S NOT AS IF THEY'RE GOING TO THROW HER A PARTY!
"OH, SHAME YOU KILLED OUR BROTHER! NO HARD FEELINGS! HAVE SOME CAKE!"
I'M SORRY, I JUST-
THEY'RE GOING TO EXECUTE HER, SIBYLLA.
WHAT?! WHEN?!

A WEEK. AT THE WEDDING.
WHAT WEDDING?
IS BROM...?
OH, GOOD JOB. WOULD YOU LIKE A PRIZE?
HE'S LETTING THEM HURT DAGNY?
APPARENTLY! I DON'T KNOW! IT'S NOT AS IF HE'S MADE A POINT OF COMING DOWN TO SEE THE PRISONERS.
BUT AN EXECUTION AT THE WEDDING, THAT'S...
THEY WANT HIM TO RENOUNCE HIS PAST, AS IF KILLING HER MAKES THEM ANY DIFFERENT.
I NEVER SHOULD HAVE LET HER SEND ME AWAY...I-

TELL ME WHERE YOU'VE COME FROM, SIBYLLA.
NICE TO MEET YOU TOO.
I TOLD YOU SHE WAS NO GOOD, PRINCESS.
TOLD YOU YOU'D BE WASTING YOUR TIME COMING DOWN HERE AND TRYING TO HAVE A CONVERSATION WITH A SABOTEUR.
NO, WAIT–I'M FROM GOOSE VALLEY. IT'S ON THE OTHER SIDE OF THE NARROW SEA.
YOU'RE HUMAN.
WHAT'S A HUMAN DOING HERE?
I WILL ASK MY OWN QUESTIONS, MOPP.
WHAT ARE YOU DOING HERE?

WELL, YOUR LITTLE FRIEND THERE CALLED THE GUARDS, AND NOW I'M IN PRISON. SO...
I WILL NOT STAY IF YOU WASTE MY TIME.
HOW IS IT THAT YOU KNOW BROM?
THEY WERE BETROTHED.

NONSENSE. THERE WAS ONLY ONE–
YOU'RE THE GIRL FROM THE PROPHECY?
YOU WERE MEANT TO BE HIS TRUE LOVE AND BREAK THE CURSE ON NORROWAY...
BUT YOU WERE UNTRUE–
WHAT.
–AND INSTEAD OF TRIUMPHING OVER THE CURSE, HE LOST HIS MEMORY...
EVERYTHING BUT HIS NAME. HE WOULD HAVE DIED IF WE HADN'T TAKEN HIM IN.
THAT IS– I WAS NOT UNTRUE!
AND WHY SHOULD I BELIEVE YOU?
YOU'VE COME HERE TO STOP THE WEDDING, HAVEN'T YOU?

DO YOU CLAIM TO LOVE HIM STILL?
ABSOLUTELY NOT. I HAVE NEVER BORNE HIM THAT SORT OF AFFECTION, PRINCESS, AND WOULD MUCH RATHER MARRY ANOTHER.
THEN WHY ARE YOU—
I WAS SEPARATED FROM—
FROM MY TRUE LOVE.
THAT'S THE GILLY YOU WERE TALKING ABOUT.
I WAS SUPPOSED TO MEET HER...
I WAS LOOKING FOR A WAY OUT OF THE WOODS AND THE NEXT THING I KNEW, I WAS BEING ASSAULTED BY YOUR PINCUSHION.
I THINK SHE'S LYING, MISS.
I HARDLY ASSAULTED HER.
MOPP, QUIET.
HE SAID HE WANTS TO SPEAK WITH YOU. HE...
HE MIGHT REMEMBER YOU.
WHAT HARM IS THERE IN THAT?

WHAT HARM INDEED!
MISS, YOU CAN'T POSSIBLY BE CONSIDERING–
MY MOTHER WOULD NEVER ALLOW IT. SHE'S BEEN SO CAREFUL WITH WHAT SHE TELLS HIM–
WHY CAREFUL? WHY BOTHER TO TELL ME AT ALL?
THE PRINCESS WANTS YOU TO SPEAK WITH HIM.
YOU SAID HE LOST HIS MEMORY, DIDN'T YOU?
DOESN'T IT FEEL STRANGE TO MARRY A MAN WHO DOES NOT KNOW HIMSELF?

I CARE FOR HIM AND HE CARES FOR ME.
HE SAID HE WISHED TO SPEAK WITH HER, AND I SAID I WOULD ADVOCATE FOR HIM. THAT IS ALL. BUT MY MOTHER–
HIS CONDITION IS SO PRECARIOUS, IF I–
WHAT IF SHE PAYS FOR THE PRIVILEGE?
YOUR MOTHER COULDN'T SAY NO TO A FAIR TRADE.
THE BRACELET. SIBYLLA, SHOW HER.
WHAT BRACELET?
...THE ONE YOU'RE WEARING, SIBYLLA. WITH THE CHARMS FROM ESBEN AND DAGNY.
OH, THIS?

THOSE CHARMS ARE–
CONTAINMENT SPELLS.
INSIDE ARE SOME OF THE GREATEST TREASURES OF NORROWAY.
REALLY? INSIDE THESE LITTLE THINGS? HOW?
YOU REALLY HAVEN'T CHANGED, HAVE YOU? MAGIC.
TAKE THEM. PLEASE LET ME SPEAK TO BROM.
PRINCESS... YOU'LL BE HONOR BOUND–

THERE'S TWO CHARMS.
TWO CHARMS, TWO CHANCES.
SO YOU'LL LET ME SPEAK TO HIM TWICE, IF I NEED TO.
FINE. YOU HAVE MY WORD.
RRRRRR
IF YOU CAN FIND A WAY TO RECOVER HIS MEMORY...
I KNOW. THEN PERHAPS ALL THREE OF US CAN GET OUT OF HERE ALIVE.

LOTA.
MOM!
I HEARD THERE WAS A VISITOR IN THE GARDEN TODAY.
YES. THE GUARDS TOOK HER AWAY.
YOU AND BROM ARE BOTH UNHARMED?

SHE SAID SHE WAS LOST IN THE WOODS. SHE'S HUMAN, NO THREAT TO US.
THE WOODS DO SEND US GIFTS FROM TIME TO TIME. GOOD AND BAD.
THOUGH, I MUST SAY, THERE IS NO GREATER TREASURE THE FOREST GAVE US THAN YOU.
WHAT DO YOU SEE, LOTA?
NORROWAY AND THE TROLL KINGDOM.
Norroway
Narrow Sea
Goose Valley
Human Realm
Glass Mountain
Old Kingdom of Norroway

I SEE OUR SOLDIERS HAVE TAKEN THE NARROW SEA TO THE BORDER OF THE HUMAN WORLD.
WHAT'S HAPPENED HERE? I THOUGHT THIS VILLAGE WELCOMED US.
viillage of Fiskeby
Narrow S
IT SEEMS FISKEBY WAS HARBORING A RESISTANCE. YOUR AUNTIE MAL HAS BEEN DEALING WITH THE REBELS.

WHY ARE THERE SO MANY SOLDIERS FOCUSED HERE?
ARE WE GOING BENEATH THE GLASS, INTO OLD NORROWAY?
WE ARE. WE HAVE BEEN, AND WE'VE BEEN FINDING STRANGE THINGS BENEATH THE MOUNTAIN.
WHAT IS THAT?
OH. THE GIRL IN THE DUNGEONS—
SHE GAVE YOU THIS?
YES. WELL. SHE... PAID ME.
PAID YOU? FOR WHAT?
LOTA, NEED I REMIND YOU THAT WE DO NOT TAKE BRIBES—

I KNOW—YOU SEE, THE THING IS, SHE SAID SHE WAS BETROTHED TO BROM.
BEFORE HE CAME HERE.
SHE'S THE GIRL.
AND YOU BELIEVED HER?
BROM SAID HE MIGHT HAVE RECOGNIZED HER.
DID HE SAY ANYTHING ELSE?
NO. BUT I THOUGHT, MAYBE IF I SPOKE TO HER, I MIGHT LEARN SOMETHING THAT COULD HELP HIM.
SHE HAD NOTHING USEFUL TO TELL YOU, DID SHE?
AND YOU DIDN'T ASK YOURSELF WHY SHE APPEARED NOW, A MERE WEEK BEFORE OUR KINGDOMS ARE SET TO BECOME ONE?

SHE HAD SEVEN YEARS TO FIND HIM. IF SHE IS WHO SHE CLAIMS TO BE, WHICH I DOUBT, SHE'S NOT COME TO HELP HIM.
SHE'S COME WITH HER OWN AGENDA.
HE WANTED TO SPEAK WITH HER! I THOUGHT, PERHAPS, IF SHE COULD BRING BACK MORE OF HIS MEMORIES...
HIS MEMORIES ARE THE ROOT OF HIS CONDITION, LOTA... DREDGING THEM UP CAN ONLY HURT HIM.
YOU KNOW THAT. WE ONLY TELL HIM WHAT WON'T BREAK HIM.
I...I PROMISED HER SHE COULD SEE HIM.
IN EXCHANGE FOR THE BRACELET, I TOLD HER SHE COULD HAVE TWO MEETINGS.
YOU DID *WHAT?!*
I'M SORRY! I DIDN'T THINK–
PING
WHUMP!

NO! YOU DIDN'T THINK!
THAT WAS FOOLISH OF YOU, LOTA. SPEAKING TO HER IN THE FIRST PLACE, MUCH LESS BEING DRAWN IN BY A SILLY BAUBLE...
BUT THERE ARE WAYS AROUND THIS.
I COULD GIVE IT BACK–
YOU MUST KEEP YOUR WORD.
SHE'LL MEET WITH HIM, BUT IT WILL BE ON OUR TERMS, AND IN A MANNER WE SEE FIT.

YOU TOLD HER ONLY THAT SHE WOULD MEET WITH HIM?
YES.
GOOD. AFTER DINNER, WE'LL HAVE HER FETCHED.
SHE CAN SPEAK AS LONG AS SHE'S ABLE.
THANK YOU, MOTHER.

BROM? SHE'S HERE.
SEND HER IN.

I DIDN'T REALIZE THERE WOULD BE AN AUDIENCE.
WE HAVE NO WAY OF CONFIRMING YOU ARE WHO YOU SAY YOU ARE.
YOU WILL NOT BE LEFT ALONE WITH HIM.
YOU CAN SIT DOWN.
NICE... CHAIRS.
I ALWAYS THOUGHT THEY SEEMED A LITTLE MUCH.

OH.
SO. YOU... KNOW ME?
THEY DIDN'T TELL YOU ANYTHING?
I BELIEVE THEY LEFT THAT UP TO YOU.
AH. WELL. MY NAME IS SIBYLLA.
YOU— WE—WERE BETROTHED.
US?
YES, US! WHAT'S THAT SUPPOSED TO MEAN?
NOTHING. WOULD YOU LIKE SOME WINE?

CHEERS, SIBYLLA.
WOW, BITTER.
MAYBE THEY DIDN'T THINK YOU WARRANTED A BETTER VINTAGE.
SO. WE WERE BETROTHED.
YES. WHEN I WAS A LITTLE GIRL, I WAS TOLD I WOULD BE THE BRIDE OF THE BLACK BULL OF NORROWAY.
SEEMS LIKE AN OFFENSIVE THING TO CALL SOMEONE.

LISTEN, I DIDN'T COME UP WITH IT.
WAIT. DIDN'T YOU KNOW ALL THAT?
I KNOW WHAT I'VE BEEN TOLD. APPARENTLY,
I WAS A LEGENDARY KNIGHT.
LEGENDARY FOR BEING MERCILESS.
MERCY IS NO FRIEND IN BATTLE— I'M SURE I WAS JUST EFFICIENT.
TRY RUTHLESS... ANYWAY, YOU CAME TO FETCH ME AFTER A WHILE.
GO ON. WHAT HAPPENED THEN? WAS I EXPECTING SOMEONE LIKE YOU? DID I LEAVE YOU?
YOU KNOW, I THINK I LIKED YOU BETTER WHEN YOU WERE A BULL.
SO I WAS AN *ACTUAL* BULL? NOT SOME SORT OF A HIDEOUS MONSTER?
NO, JUST A GIANT BULL. ROUND. FOUR LEGS. HORNS. I DRANK WINE OUT OF YOUR EAR.
YOUR PERSONALITY WAS WHAT MADE YOU THE HIDEOUS MONSTER.

I'VE DREAMT OF WANDERING THE COUNTRYSIDE AS A BULL...
I DREAMT OF A MAGPIE-
BRINGING YOU A RIBBON?
YES... YES!
BUT, THERE WAS A CURSE PLACED ON MY KINGDOM...

YOUR CURSE, YOU MEAN.
YOUR FAULT. YOU DIDN'T BREAK IT. YOU COULDN'T FORGIVE...
MY CURSE?
WHO COULDN'T I FORGIVE?
SIBYLLA-
FORGIVE...
SIBYLLA?

LOTA...?
I'M HERE, BROM.
I FEEL SO FOGGY...
YOU... YOU FELL ASLEEP AFTER DINNER.
AH...
YOU DON'T REMEMBER?
...NO. I MUST HAVE DREAMED... I THOUGHT... SIBYLLA...
YOU'RE BURNING UP.

I FEEL STRANGE, LOTA. I FEEL LIKE I'M OUT OF MY OWN BODY. LIKE I DON'T KNOW MYSELF.
WHAT IF WE DRESS YOU IN YOUR FINERY? MAYBE YOU'LL FEEL YOURSELF AGAIN.

WHAT IS THIS?
IT WAS YOURS FROM WHEN WE FOUND YOU.
MAYBE IT COULD REMIND YOU--?
WHOSE BLOOD-
I DON'T KNOW.

IS THIS WHO I WAS THEN? A MAN OF BLEEDING AND BLOODSTAINS?
...MOTHER'S TOLD US BOTH TALES OF WHAT NORROWAY USED TO BE.
AYE...
WE'RE LUCKY SHE TOOK US BOTH IN.
I WAS A CHILD, OF COURSE.
MAYBE THAT MADE IT EASIER FOR ME.
WHO WAS I, LOTA? HAS SHE TOLD YOU? DOES SHE KNOW WHO I WAS?
I FEEL LIKE IT'S THERE. IT'S ON THE TIP OF MY TONGUE, SOMETHING I CAN'T SHAKE...
I FEEL LIKE-
YOU'RE ALL RIGHT, BROM.
I'M SORRY, I THOUGHT THIS WOULD HELP.

I WAS A PRINCE. I WAS A PRINCE OF NORROWAY, AND A PRINCE IS THE KINGDOM.
I WAS NORROWAY, I WAS... THIS BLOOD, I WAS...
MY FAULT. *MY FAULT!*
NO, BROM. NO, NO. NO, LOVE.
STAY WITH ME, ALL RIGHT?
I COULDN'T FORGIVE...
I COULDN'T FORGIVE— *AGH!*
BREATHE! BROM! STAY HERE WITH ME!
IT'S GONE! SEE? IT'S GONE NOW.
IT DOESN'T MATTER ANYMORE. IT'S JUST AN OLD SHIRT.
BROM!
YOU CAN'T JUST THROW IT AWAY! YOU CAN'T THROW IT AWAY!
IT WILL ALWAYS BE STAINED, LOTA, IT WILL–
NO! NO. WE'LL...WE'LL TAKE IT AND WE'LL CLEAN IT. LOOK. LOOK!

WE'LL WASH THE BLOOD FROM IT, AND IT WILL JUST BE A SHIRT AGAIN. JUST A SHIRT, AND YOU, JUST A MAN.
A NEW START, ALL RIGHT? NO MORE WORRYING ABOUT WHO YOU WERE, OR WHAT YOU WERE. JUST WHO YOU'LL BE.
WHO...
WITH ME.
WITH YOU.
...AND IF IT'S TOO STAINED?
IF IT BLEEDS ONTO EVERYTHING IT TOUCHES? WHAT THEN?
IT WON'T.
ANYTHING CAN BE CLEANED.
WHOSE BLOOD-

HOW'S THIS? WE'LL MARRY ONCE YOU'VE A CLEAN SHIRT, AND NOT BEFORE. NO STAINS ON OUR MARRIAGE.
A CLEAN SHIRT... NO STAINS.
IS THAT WHAT YOU WANT?
A CLEAN SHIRT, A CLEAN START.
A CLEAN START.

~ZZZZZZZZZZZZZZZZZZ *PING* ZZZZ
~ZZZZZZZ *PING* ZZZZZZZZZ
~ZZZZZZZZZ
PING
~ZZZZZZZZZZZZZ
PING ~ZZZZZZZ *PING*
~ZZZZZZZZZZZZZZZZZZ
~ZZZ *PING*
~ZZ-WHA-??
ABOUT TIME! WHAT HAPPENED UP THERE?
I FEEL AWFUL.
I DON'T CARE. WHAT HAPPENED?
I DON'T KNOW.
YOU DON'T KNOW!?
YOU CAME BACK UNCONSCIOUS, I'VE BEEN THROWING ROCKS AT YOU FOR HOURS NOW, AND YOU TELL ME YOU DON'T KNOW WHAT HAPPENED!?
I THINK THE WINE WAS DRUGGED...

YOU DRANK THE WINE? YOU **NEVER** DRINK THE WINE! YOU **NEVER** TAKE THE FOOD!
NOBODY TOLD ME THAT! NOBODY TOLD ME THE RULES!
THEY DIDN'T TELL ME SEVEN YEARS AGO, AND THEY SURE AS **HELL** DIDN'T TELL ME TODAY!
YOU'VE WASTED ONE OF OUR CHANCES, SIBYLLA. NOW WE HAVE ONE LEFT.
SO WHY DON'T YOU GO UP THERE? YOU KNEW HIM TOO.
YOU TWO HATED EACH OTHER SO MUCH, I'M SURE THERE'S SOMETHING YOU COULD SAY TO JOG HIS MEMORY.

I WOULD LOVE TO, BUT I'M NOT THE ONE WHO MADE THE TRADE,
SO UNLESS YOU HAVE A BETTER IDEA-
WHAT IF I COULD BUY YOU A CHANCE?
WITH WHAT?
SIBYLLA, THAT'S A SEASHELL.
HOW SHOULD I KNOW! IF RICHES CAN BE TUCKED INTO TINY CHARMS, WHY NOT A SEASHELL?
THIS NECKLACE IS IMPORTANT TO ME, ANYWAY, SO THAT SHOULD BE WORTH SOMETHING.
IT ISN'T.
IT'S SO EASY TO BE CRUEL WHEN YOU HAVE ALL THE INFORMATION, JUST THROWING ME SCRAPS WHENEVER YOU FEEL LIKE IT.

SO HIGH AND MIGHTY.
"LOOK AT ME, I'M DHOW AND I'M SO SMART, I HAVE EVERYTHING ALL FIGURED OUT, AND I'M MEAN TO EVERYONE BECAUSE THEY DON'T KNOW ALL THE THINGS THAT I KNOW."
I LOST MY TRUE LOVE, AND MY BIRD IS MISSING, AND A THOUSAND OTHER THINGS!
YOU'RE SO TERRIBLE ALL THE TIME!
BUT GUESS WHAT!? YOU'RE LOCKED IN A DUNGEON JUST LIKE ME, SO YOU'RE NOT THE ONLY ONE HAVING A HARD TIME, OK!?
AND YOU HAVE ALL THE WITS OF A TURNIP!
WELL LOOK WHO'S HERE.

YOU DRUGGED ME.
I'M SORRY–
YOU'RE SORRY YOU DRUGGED ME?
I DIDN'T KNOW THE WINE WAS DRUGGED! I DIDN'T KNOW!
OH, THAT MAKES IT ALL BETTER, DOESN'T IT?
I JUST... I DON'T THINK IT WAS FAIR...

WHY SHOULD I CARE WHAT YOU THINK IS FAIR? WHAT DOES YOUR APOLOGY CHANGE? WHAT DID YOU COME DOWN HERE FOR, A PAT ON THE BACK?
NO, I... THE QUEEN ORDERED THE WINE DRUGGED.
I KEPT MY WORD. I NEEDED YOU TO KNOW I KEPT MY WORD.
CONVENIENT.
NEVERMIND. I SHOULDN'T HAVE COME.
PROBABLY NOT, NO.
WE'RE LEAVING, MOPP...

WAIT! I HAVE ONE MORE MEETING. TAKE ME.
WHAT, NOW? I CAN'T.
WHY, DO YOU NEED TIME TO MAKE SURE THE WINE IS DRUGGED?
NO! I–
THEN YOU'RE AFRAID I'LL RUIN YOUR PRECIOUS WEDDING, IS THAT IT?
NO–! IT'S– IT'S BROM. HE'S– IT WOULD HARM HIM– I'VE TOLD YOU HE HAS EPISODES, HE...
HIS MEMORIES ARE TOO MUCH.
TELL ME EXACTLY WHAT HE REMEMBERS.
THAT NORROWAY WAS A BAD KINGDOM, THAT HE WAS CURSED AS A RESULT OF THE KING AND TURNED INTO A BEAST.
HE KNOWS THERE WAS A MAIDEN WHO WAS PROPHESIZED TO HELP HIM BREAK THE CURSE, BUT SHE FAILED, AND THAT IS WHY HE ISN'T WHOLE.
WHY IS IT ALWAYS MY FAULT!?

ISN'T IT?
WE'VE BEEN OVER THIS!
JUST TAKE ME TO HIM. KEEP YOUR PROMISE, AND TAKE ME TO HIM.
I WON'T.
I DON'T CARE IF HE REMEMBERS ME. BUT WHAT KIND OF A PERSON WOULD YOU BE IF YOU KEPT HIS MEMORIES FROM HIM? HOW CAN HE AGREE TO MARRY YOU IF HE DOESN'T EVEN KNOW WHO HE IS? HE CAN'T CONSENT TO THAT!
YOU DON'T KNOW WHAT YOU'RE TALKING ABOUT!
YOU GAVE YOUR WORD. TWO MEETINGS. YOU'RE BOUND TO A SECOND.
SOME PRINCESS YOU ARE, DODGING YOUR OBLIGATIONS.
I'M NOT– IT'S JUST...

HE'S SLEEPING RIGHT NOW. IF WE COULD JUST WAIT—
NO WAITING. WE'LL WAKE HIM UP. IF YOU'RE TRULY BOUND TO YOUR WORD, THEN YOU'LL TAKE ME *NOW.*
ONE MORE MEETING. FIVE MINUTES.
YOU HAVE TO BE VERY, VERY QUIET. IF ANYONE KNEW—
I WON'T MAKE A SOUND.

WAKE UP, BROM!
WAKE UP AND LOOK AT ME!
BROM!
SIBYLLA...
THUMP-
STAY OUT OF THIS!

BROM, I TRIED TO SAVE YOU BUT I COULDN'T. I FELL DOWN THE GLASS, AND I SERVED A BLACKSMITH FOR SEVEN YEARS, TO LEARN HOW TO MAKE THE SHOES TO CLIMB BACK UP.

I MAY NOT HAVE CLIMBED THE GLASS FOR YOU, BROM, BUT I'M HERE NOW AND I WON'T LET THEM USE YOU. I WON'T LET THEM KILL DAGNY AND CLAIM IT CHANGES THE PAST. I KNOW YOU WOULDN'T WANT THAT, I KNOW YOU WOULDN'T LET YOUR SISTER DIE.

SO WAKE UP, BROM! DON'T LET YOURSELF BE A PAWN FOR KINGS AND QUEENS ANY LONGER!

YOU!
YOU TRICKED ME!
NO, I-
HOW CAN YOU CLAIM TO CARE FOR HIM IF YOU'RE THE ONE LETTING THIS HAPPEN!?
LIAR!

LATER...
IT'S LUCKY I GAVE HIM SOMETHING TO HELP HIM SLEEP. THAT GIRL, CARRYING ON LIKE THAT...
LOTA, WHAT WERE YOU THINKING?
I-
WE KEEP OUR WORD ON OUR OWN TERMS. WE DON'T BEND TO THE WILLS OF OTHERS. IF YOU'RE TO BE QUEEN SOMEDAY, YOU NEED TO START ACTING THE PART.
I KNOW...
WE'LL HAVE HER TAKEN CARE OF.
WHAT?
SHE BEGUILED YOU AGAIN, THIS TIME INTO TAKING HER TO HIS ROOM. WHO KNOWS WHAT SHE HAD PLANNED.
NO MATTER. SHE'LL BE ANOTHER PIECE OF HIS SORDID HISTORY WIPED CLEAN AFTER THE WEDDING.
NO, SHE DIDN'T-

SHE'S A DANGER, DON'T YOU SEE THAT? NOT JUST TO HIM, BUT TO EVERYONE. TO THE KINGDOM. SHE'S NOT YOUR FRIEND, LOTA.
I NEVER CLAIMED SHE WAS MY FRIEND, BUT I DON'T THINK SHE DESERVES–
YOU KNOW NOTHING ABOUT HER. SHE WILL BE PUT TO DEATH ALONG WITH THE OTHER PRISONERS.
MAL, SISTER, COME HERE.
HOW'S MY FAVORITE NIECE?
ONLY NIECE.

MAKES THE COMPETITION EASY, DOESN'T IT?
TELL MY ERRANT DAUGHTER WHAT YOU TOLD ME, MAL.
THE GIRL IS FROM FISKEBY. SHE ESCAPED AFTER KILLING ONE OF MY SOLDIERS, CLIMBED RIGHT UP THE GLASS.
YOU REMEMBER KETTLE, DON'T YOU?
SAUCEPOT'S HUSBAND...?
THAT'S THE ONE.
DID YOU KNOW SHE CAN SPEAK? DID YOU KNOW SHE USED ***WORDS*** TO KILL HIM? HE WAS CRUSHED BENEATH A TREE LIMB.
BUT YOU CAN'T USE ***WORDS*** IF YOU INTEND HARM. THEY WON'T WORK–

HUMANS AREN'T BOUND BY OUR LAWS. SHE CAN SPEAK TO HARM, SHE CAN BREAK HER PROMISES.
THERE'S NOTHING STOPPING HER.
SHE CAN LIE AS IT SUITS HER. SHE CAN WEAVE WHATEVER FICTION FITS HER DESIRE.
HUMANS ARE TRICKSY THINGS, MANIPULATIVE THINGS.
THERE'S A GOOD REASON OUR WORLDS ARE KEPT SEPARATE...
I'M SORRY YOU HAD TO LEARN THAT THIS WAY, LOTA.
...SHE TOLD ME IT WAS UNFAIR TO MARRY HIM.
UNFAIR HOW?

BECAUSE HE DOESN'T KNOW WHO HE IS!
THAT DOESN'T MATTER, LOTA. HE'S NEVER GOING TO REMEMBER.
HE MIGHT! AND WHAT THEN? WHAT IF HE'S NEVER ABLE TO BREAK THE CURSE?
HE WON'T, LOTA.
WHEN WE FOUND HIM, HE WAS A MESS.
THE ONLY WAY TO CALM HIM, THE ONLY WAY TO PUT HIM AT EASE, WAS TO TAKE HIS MEMORIES.
PERHAPS IF THE CURSE HAD BEEN FULLY BROKEN THIS WOULDN'T HAVE BEEN NECESSARY, BUT...
IT'S BETTER FOR BROM IF THAT PART OF HIMSELF IS LOCKED AWAY.
THAT WAY HE CAN FORGET THE THINGS HE'S DONE, THE THINGS NORROWAY HAS DONE. HE CAN FORGET THE CURSE.

YOU TOOK THEM–? BUT–NO!
WE CAN'T KEEP HIS MEMORIES FROM HIM!
WHO WOULD I BE WITHOUT MY MEMORIES? WITHOUT KNOWING WHERE I HAD BEEN, OR WHAT I HAD LIVED THROUGH?
THOSE DON'T BELONG TO YOU!
I'VE MADE THE CHOICE THAT'S BEST FOR HIM, JUST AS I MAKE THE BEST CHOICES FOR OUR KINGDOM.
SOMETIMES WE ARE FORCED TO CHOOSE.
LOTA, LOVE, HE WOULD GO MAD BENEATH THEIR WEIGHT.
BUT THEY BELONG TO HIM! WHY WOULD YOU LET ME THINK HE WAS BROKEN WHEN ***WE'RE*** THE ONES WHO ACTUALLY BROKE HIM?
LOTA, HE WAS BROKEN LONG BEFORE HE CAME TO US. THIS WILL MEND HIM, MOLD HIM INTO THE PRINCE HE SHOULD HAVE BEEN.
THAT ISN'T OUR RIGHT! IF IT WASN'T FATE'S DECISION–
THE QUEEN KNOWS WHAT SHE'S DOING. YOU HAVE TO TRUST HER.
IF IT AILS YOU SO GREATLY THEN PERHAPS, AFTER THE WEDDING, WE COULD...
GIVE HIM A FEW OF HIS MEMORIES BACK.
A LITTLE BIT AT A TIME.
THERE'S NOT GOING TO BE A WEDDING!

WHAT?
THERE–
THERE ISN'T... WE AREN'T GOING TO BE MARRIED.
NEED I REMIND YOU THAT THIS WEDDING IS GOING TO REPAIR HUNDREDS OF YEARS OF DAMAGE?
THAT IT WILL END ALL OF THE TERRITORY DISPUTES WE ARE CURRENTLY FACING?
NEED I REMIND YOU, DAUGHTER, THAT THIS MARRIAGE WILL SAVE HUNDREDS, IF NOT THOUSANDS, OF TROLL LIVES?
I TOLD HIM WE...WE WOULDN'T MARRY UNTIL HE HAD A CLEAN SHIRT.
A CLEAN SHIRT? WHAT ARE YOU GOING ON ABOUT?

HIS SHIRT, THE ONE YOU FOUND HIM IN...
WE WON'T BE MARRIED UNTIL THE STAINS ARE CLEANED FROM IT.
YOU NAÏVE GIRL.
THAT SHIRT WILL NEVER COME CLEAN, LOTA. IT'S AS STAINED AND CURSED AS THE REST OF HIM.
THAT'S THE BARGAIN I MADE.
TELL ME EXACTLY WHAT YOU SAID.
I SAID 'WE'LL MARRY ONCE YOU'VE A CLEAN SHIRT.'
THAT'S WHAT I SAID.
'A' CLEAN SHIRT? NOT 'THIS' SHIRT?
YES... 'A' SHIRT. WHY?

YOU'LL WASH HIS SHIRT AT THE WEDDING. WE'LL PUT A CLEAN SHIRT IN THE BASIN WITH THE STAINED ONE, AND YOU'LL PRESENT HIM WITH THE CLEAN ONE. THE WEDDING GOES ON.
BUT THAT'S NOT WHAT I MEANT-
YOU'LL BE KEEPING YOUR WORD.
BUT IT'S ONLY A HALF-TRUTH.
AND YOU MUST LEARN TO USE HALF-TRUTHS IF YOU'RE EVER TO BECOME QUEEN.
IT'S LATE, LOTA. I THINK IT'S BEST YOU SLEEP ON THIS.

I... I DON'T WANT TO DO THIS.
IT DOESN'T FEEL RIGHT.
WHEN DID MY OWN DAUGHTER BECOME SO UNGRATEFUL?
THIS IS HOW IT WILL BE DONE. BROM WILL GET HIS CLEAN SHIRT, I WILL KEEP HIS MEMORIES, AND YOU WILL OBEY YOUR QUEEN.
MOM, I–
DO NOT DARE ARGUE WITH ME NOW, GIRL. YOU HAVE ALREADY DISOBEYED ME.
BUT–
SELFISH CHILD! YOU WILL DO THIS, LOTA. THIS IS YOUR DUTY AS MY DAUGHTER AND AS THE PRINCESS OF THIS LAND.
THIS IS NOT ABOUT YOUR MISGIVINGS. THIS IS ABOUT OUR PEOPLE, AND YOU ARE NOT TO PUT YOURSELF ABOVE THEM!
HAVE I MADE MYSELF CLEAR?

YES, MOTHER.
MAL, TAKE HER TO HER QUARTERS.
MY QUEEN.

CLANG
GILLY, I'M SO SORRY...

SIBYLLA, IS THAT YOU?
DAGNY?
DHOW TOLD ME YOU WERE HERE, I-
ARE YOU ALL RIGHT?
WELL MET, SISTER.
WE DIDN'T BREAK THE CURSE.
OF COURSE, YOU KNEW THAT.
BUT- IF WE HAD, THEN MAYBE-
I'M SO SORRY.
I BEAR YOU NO GRUDGE FOR THAT, SIBYLLA.

MAYBE YOU OUGHT TO.
I TRIED TO SPEAK WITH BROM, BUT THE FIRST TIME THEY DRUGGED US AND THE SECOND TIME HE WOULDN'T AWAKEN.
I THOUGHT—
IT WAS STUPID OF ME TO THINK THAT MAYBE THIS WAS A STORY I WAS MEANT TO FINISH AND NOW...
NOW I'VE RUINED EVERYTHING.
YOU HAVEN'T RUINED ANYTHING. ALL OF THESE PIECES WERE IN PLACE LONG BEFORE YOU BECAME INVOLVED.
I JUST THOUGHT—
THIS ISN'T SOMETHING ANY ONE PERSON CAN FIX, SIBYLLA. NOT THE CURSE, NOT OUR LIVES, NOT OUR CRIMES OR OUR PUNISHMENTS.
BUT YOU DON'T DESERVE TO BE PUNISHED!
I AGREE.
AND I HAVE NO REGRETS FOR WHAT I HAVE DONE, OR THE LIFE I HAVE LIVED. I REGRET ONLY THAT I HAVE BEEN MADE THE VILLAIN IN SOMEONE ELSE'S STORY, AND THE VOICE THEY HAVE USED TO TELL THEIR TALE HAS BEEN LOUDER THAN MINE.
BUT I WOULD DO IT ALL OVER AGAIN, NO MATTER THE RESULT.

CREEEEEEEKK
SIBYLLA...
WHAT DO YOU WANT?
I WANT TO SPEAK TO YOU...
THEN YOU SHOULDN'T HAVE LIED TO ME.
AND YOU SHOULDN'T HAVE MURDERED KETTLE!

I DIDN'T MURDER ANYONE!
AND I DIDN'T LIE TO YOU! BUT HOW CAN I BELIEVE ANYTHING YOU SAY?
YOU CAN LIE ABOUT WHATEVER YOU WANT TO.
IS THAT IT, THEN? YOU'VE COME ALL THE WAY DOWN HERE JUST TO ACCUSE ME?
NO, I–
TELL ME THE TRUTH. WHY DIDN'T YOU BREAK THE CURSE?
BECAUSE THE CURSE WAS NOT MY RESPONSIBILITY! IT WAS JUST SOME... ARBITRARY BIT OF PHRASING.
"A SWORD, A SHIELD, AND ONE BELOVED."
MAYBE IF WE HAD LOVED EACH OTHER.
HE NEVER LOVED YOU?
YOU KNOW, THAT'S REALLY NOT THE POINT HERE.

BUT IT IS THE POINT! IF ONLY TRUE LOVE COULD BREAK THE CURSE, THEN–
PLEASE DON'T TELL ME YOU THINK YOU'RE GOING TO BREAK THE CURSE AND BRING HIS LOST MEMORIES BACK WITH TRUE LOVE.
NO, OF COURSE NOT! BROM DIDN'T LOSE HIS MEMORIES. THE QUEEN TOOK THEM. SHE SAID THEY WERE A DANGER TO HIM, AND I THOUGHT IF I COULD UNDERSTAND THE CURSE THAT...
MAYBE IF I COULD BREAK IT–
THERE'S NOTHING TO UNDERSTAND. LOVE IS THE LEAST OF BROM'S PROBLEMS. THE KING COMMANDED BROM TO SACRIFICE THE PRINCESS TO THE OLD ONE, SO THAT THE TWO OF THEM WOULD HAVE MORE POWER. THAT'S WHY NORROWAY WAS CURSED.
THAT'S NOT THE STORY. THE KING SACRIFICED HIS ***OWN*** DAUGHTER FOR THE POWER THE OLD ONE WOULD BRING HIM. BROM WAS THE PRINCE, WHY WOULD HE HAVE KILLED–

HIS SISTER. THE KING'S DAUGHTER WAS HIS SISTER.
BRISE.
SHE'D ALWAYS LOVED HIM BEST OF ALL OF US. SHE TRUSTED HIM.
HOW COULD HE--?
HE LONGED TO BE A LOYAL AND OBEDIENT KNIGHT. HE LONGED FOR THE LOVE OF OUR FATHER.
IS IT NOT THE SAME REASON YOU TURN A BLIND EYE TO THE ACTIONS OF YOUR QUEEN?
CORRUPTION STARTS SMALL, BUT HER LOVE MEANS SO MUCH TO YOU. YOU IGNORE THE SIGNS.

MY MOTHER IS ONLY DOING WHAT'S BEST FOR THE KINGDOM.
FOR THE TROLL KINGDOM! OUR VILLAGE WAS ON THE BRINK OF RUIN AND STARVATION.
THE PEOPLE AREN'T EMBRACING THE TROLLS, THEY'RE AFRAID OF THEM.
THAT ISN'T TRUE!
THEY BURNED DOWN DAGNY'S PALACE–
SHE KILLED MY UNCLE!
I PROTECTED MY OWN LIFE.
LOTA, YOU CAN HELP US. JUST... LET US GO.

I CAN'T.
YOUR MOTHER TOOK BROM'S MEMORIES AND NOW HE HAS EPISODES. THOSE MUST BE RELATED SOMEHOW.
YOU DON'T UNDERSTAND. SHE'S MY MOTHER. I HAVE TO TRUST THAT WHAT SHE'S DOING IS THE RIGHT THING.
SHE CARES FOR HER PEOPLE, FOR ALL OF THE TROLL KINGDOM. SHE CARES FOR ME. I WON'T BETRAY HER.
SHE'S USING YOU, MARRYING YOU TO A MURDERER!
YOU DON'T KNOW WHAT YOU'RE TALKING ABOUT!
HE'S NOT— YOU DON'T KNOW ANYTHING! YOU JUST— MAL TOLD ME HUMANS WERE MANIPULATIVE... BROM ISN'T...
HE WOULD NEVER HURT SOMEONE HE LOVED.
YOU'RE A LIAR! THEY'RE RIGHT TO EXECUTE YOU!

WHAT!?
A LIAR AND A KILLER BOTH. THEY'RE RIGHT.
NO, I— PLEASE, LOTA, YOU CAN'T—
I HAVE TO GET OUT OF HERE— I HAVE TO—
LOTA!
LOTA!
SLAM

YOU WEREN'T DOWN THERE WITH THAT GIRL AGAIN, WERE YOU, MISS?
I JUST WANT TO GO TO BED, MOPP.
I HOPE YOU'RE NOT PLANNING ANYTHING–
I'M NOT. GO AWAY, MOPP.

MISS, YOU KNOW I CARE FOR YOU AS IF YOU WERE MY OWN HOGLET.
THINGS SEEM A LITTLE BLEAK NOW, BUT THEY WILL GET BETTER–
YOU'VE MADE A FOOL OF ME!
WHAT? TO THAT WRETCHED HUMAN GIRL?
YES, TO HER AND TO MY OWN MOTHER! NO ONE TRUSTS ME TO KNOW WHAT I'M DOING, OR TO DO THE RIGHT THING!
EVEN WHEN I'M TRYING TO KEEP MY OATHS, EVEN WHEN I'M TRYING–
I'M JUST TRYING TO BE THE DAUGHTER MOM EXPECTS, EVEN THOUGH– EVEN IF–
LOTA–
GET AWAY FROM ME!
ARE YOU GOING TO BE ABLE TO KEEP THEM IN LINE?

I'M DOING WHAT I CAN. THERE'S MORE OF THEM EVERY DAY.
THEY'VE MADE A MARTYR OF THAT WOMAN, BEATRICE DHOW...
WE SHOULD EASE UP ON THE TRADE RESTRICTIONS.
NO. I DO NOT LONG TO BE CRUEL, BUT IF WE LET THESE UPRISINGS GO UNCHECKED...

KILL THEM ALL IF YOU HAVE TO.
HOW'S THE RESEARCH BENEATH THE GLASS COMING?
ANOTHER TROOP OF SOLDIERS IS MISSING.
HOW MANY THIS TIME?
FIFTY.
KEEP PRESSING FORWARD. THERE'S SOMETHING IN THERE... SOMETHING AT THE HEART OF THE OLD PALACE.
IF IT WAS THE KEY TO THE KING'S POWER, I WANT IT.
I WOULD LIKE TO SPEAK FREELY, AS YOUR SISTER.
IF YOU MUST.
THERE MAY COME A POINT WHEN THE COST BECOMES TOO HIGH.
I DON'T THINK YOU SHOULD KEEP DIGGING IN THIS, NOG. THE CURSE–
DON'T TELL ME YOU'RE AFRAID OF THE CURSE?
THAT WAS SOMETHING THEY BROUGHT DOWN ON THEIR OWN HEADS.
IT ISN'T OURS TO BEAR.

YOU HAVEN'T SEEN—
WE WILL FIND WHAT THERE IS TO BE FOUND, MAL, AND WE WILL TAKE IT. NO MATTER THE COST.
I EXPECT YOUR UNCONDITIONAL SUPPORT ON THIS.
YES, MY QUEEN.
MISTRESS—
I NEVER WANT TO SEE YOU AGAIN, MOPP. NOT IN THE PALACE, NOT AT THE WEDDING.
LEAVE ME.
Sniffle

LOTA! YOU'RE MEANT TO BE IN YOUR ROOMS.
AUNTIE MAL!
YOU WENT TO SEE THAT GIRL AGAIN.
I TOLD HER THE FATE THAT AWAITED HER.
YOU NEEDN'T HAVE DONE THAT.
WE ARE NOT DELIBERATELY CRUEL.
I WENT TO ASK HER ABOUT THE CURSE, AUNTIE.
IS IT TRUE...? HIS OWN SISTER?
NORROWAY WAS THE DARK BEATING HEART OF EVIL, LOTA.
OR DON'T YOU REMEMBER WHAT THEIR ARMIES DID TO YOUR FAMILY?

WHY AM I MARRYING HIM? WHY WOULD MOTHER--?
HE WAS NEVER HIS OWN MAN, ONLY THE KING'S DOG.
HE WOULD HAVE OBEYED ANY ORDER. WITHOUT HIS MEMORIES, WITHOUT HIS KING, HE'S TOOTHLESS.
SHE WAITED SEVEN LONG YEARS TO SEE TO THAT.
AND IF HE TROUBLES YOU, SHE'LL FIND A WAY FOR YOU TO BE RID OF HIM.
WHAT?
IF HE PROVED TO BE A RISK, LOTA, HE WOULD BE DISPOSED OF.
HE DOESN'T MEAN ANYTHING TO HER THEN, DOES HE? HE'S JUST A MEANS TO AN END.
AND THE... THE EXECUTIONS ARE FOR REVENGE AND NOTHING MORE.
IS IT ALL JUST A FARCE THEN, THIS WEDDING? SHE'S USING THE TWO OF US--
NO, LOTA. SHE LOVES YOU AS A DAUGHTER, DO NOT EVER DOUBT THAT.
BUT--
IF YOU BELIEVE NOTHING ELSE, BELIEVE THAT.

COME ON, LET'S GET YOU BACK TO BED.
MOTHER HATED NORROWAY, DIDN'T SHE?
AYE. WE ALL DID.
...THEN WHY IS SHE SENDING SOLDIERS BENEATH THE GLASS?
YOU'RE A LITTLE SPY THEN, ARE YOU?
I WOULDN'T ASK THOSE QUESTIONS OF THE QUEEN, LOTA. THEY'RE NOT THINGS YOU'RE MEANT TO KNOW.
BUT WHAT GOOD WILL COME OF ANYTHING WE FIND THERE?
HOW CAN SHE EXPECT TO USE IT? IF THE WEDDING IS NOTHING BUT POLITICS, IF–
TRUST YOUR MOTHER, LOTA, AND KNOW THAT SHE LOVES THE KINGDOM BEST OF ALL OF US.
SHE'S ONLY DOING WHAT SHE BELIEVES IS RIGHT.

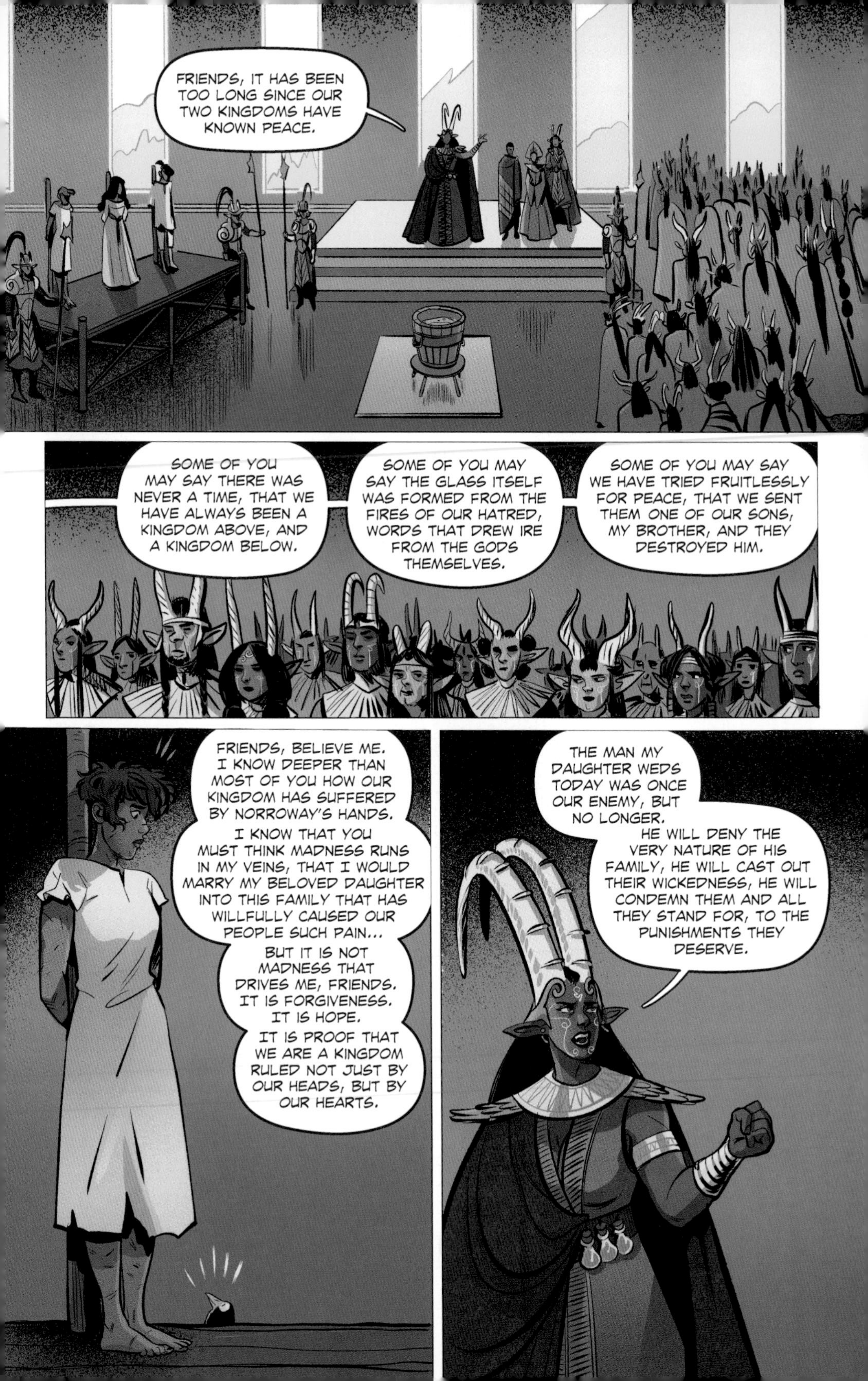
FRIENDS, IT HAS BEEN TOO LONG SINCE OUR TWO KINGDOMS HAVE KNOWN PEACE.
SOME OF YOU MAY SAY THERE WAS NEVER A TIME, THAT WE HAVE ALWAYS BEEN A KINGDOM ABOVE, AND A KINGDOM BELOW.
SOME OF YOU MAY SAY THE GLASS ITSELF WAS FORMED FROM THE FIRES OF OUR HATRED, WORDS THAT DREW IRE FROM THE GODS THEMSELVES.
SOME OF YOU MAY SAY WE HAVE TRIED FRUITLESSLY FOR PEACE, THAT WE SENT THEM ONE OF OUR SONS, MY BROTHER, AND THEY DESTROYED HIM.
FRIENDS, BELIEVE ME. I KNOW DEEPER THAN MOST OF YOU HOW OUR KINGDOM HAS SUFFERED BY NORROWAY'S HANDS.
I KNOW THAT YOU MUST THINK MADNESS RUNS IN MY VEINS, THAT I WOULD MARRY MY BELOVED DAUGHTER INTO THIS FAMILY THAT HAS WILLFULLY CAUSED OUR PEOPLE SUCH PAIN...
BUT IT IS NOT MADNESS THAT DRIVES ME, FRIENDS. IT IS FORGIVENESS. IT IS HOPE.
IT IS PROOF THAT WE ARE A KINGDOM RULED NOT JUST BY OUR HEADS, BUT BY OUR HEARTS.
THE MAN MY DAUGHTER WEDS TODAY WAS ONCE OUR ENEMY, BUT NO LONGER.
HE WILL DENY THE VERY NATURE OF HIS FAMILY, HE WILL CAST OUT THEIR WICKEDNESS, HE WILL CONDEMN THEM AND ALL THEY STAND FOR, TO THE PUNISHMENTS THEY DESERVE.

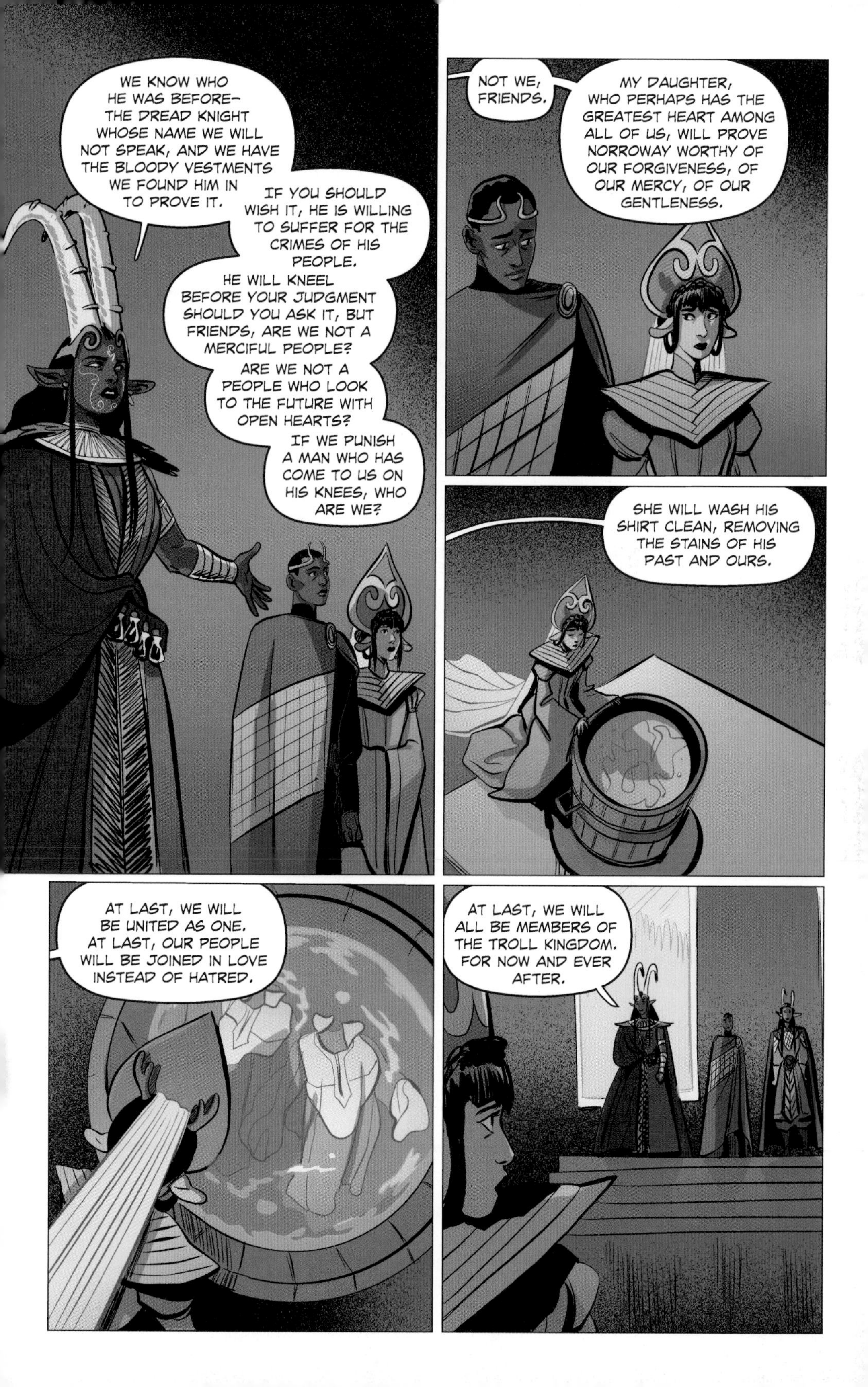
WE KNOW WHO HE WAS BEFORE— THE DREAD KNIGHT WHOSE NAME WE WILL NOT SPEAK, AND WE HAVE THE BLOODY VESTMENTS WE FOUND HIM IN TO PROVE IT.
IF YOU SHOULD WISH IT, HE IS WILLING TO SUFFER FOR THE CRIMES OF HIS PEOPLE.
HE WILL KNEEL BEFORE YOUR JUDGMENT SHOULD YOU ASK IT, BUT FRIENDS, ARE WE NOT A MERCIFUL PEOPLE?
ARE WE NOT A PEOPLE WHO LOOK TO THE FUTURE WITH OPEN HEARTS?
IF WE PUNISH A MAN WHO HAS COME TO US ON HIS KNEES, WHO ARE WE?
NOT WE, FRIENDS.
MY DAUGHTER, WHO PERHAPS HAS THE GREATEST HEART AMONG ALL OF US, WILL PROVE NORROWAY WORTHY OF OUR FORGIVENESS, OF OUR MERCY, OF OUR GENTLENESS.
SHE WILL WASH HIS SHIRT CLEAN, REMOVING THE STAINS OF HIS PAST AND OURS.
AT LAST, WE WILL BE UNITED AS ONE. AT LAST, OUR PEOPLE WILL BE JOINED IN LOVE INSTEAD OF HATRED.
AT LAST, WE WILL ALL BE MEMBERS OF THE TROLL KINGDOM. FOR NOW AND EVER AFTER.

THIS IS YOUR SHIRT, BROM, AND IT WILL NEVER COME CLEAN! WE CAN'T WASH AWAY OUR PAST!
DO YOU WANT TO KNOW WHY YOU HAVE NO MEMORIES?
SNIP!

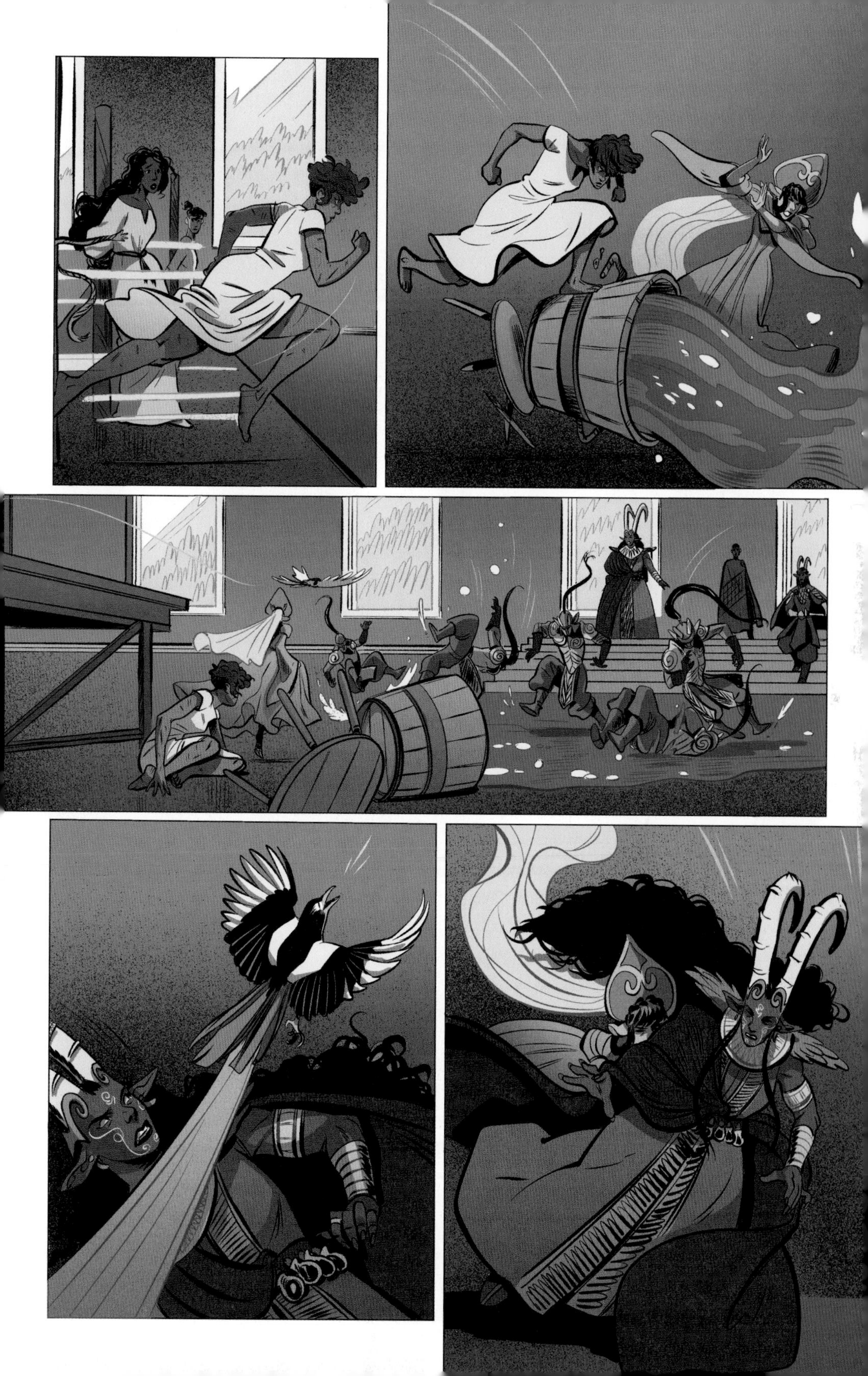

LOTA-
IF I'M TO MARRY A MONSTER, LET ME KNOW THE TRUTH OF IT! LET EVERYONE KNOW THE TRUTH OF IT!

LET'S GO! GRAB HIM!

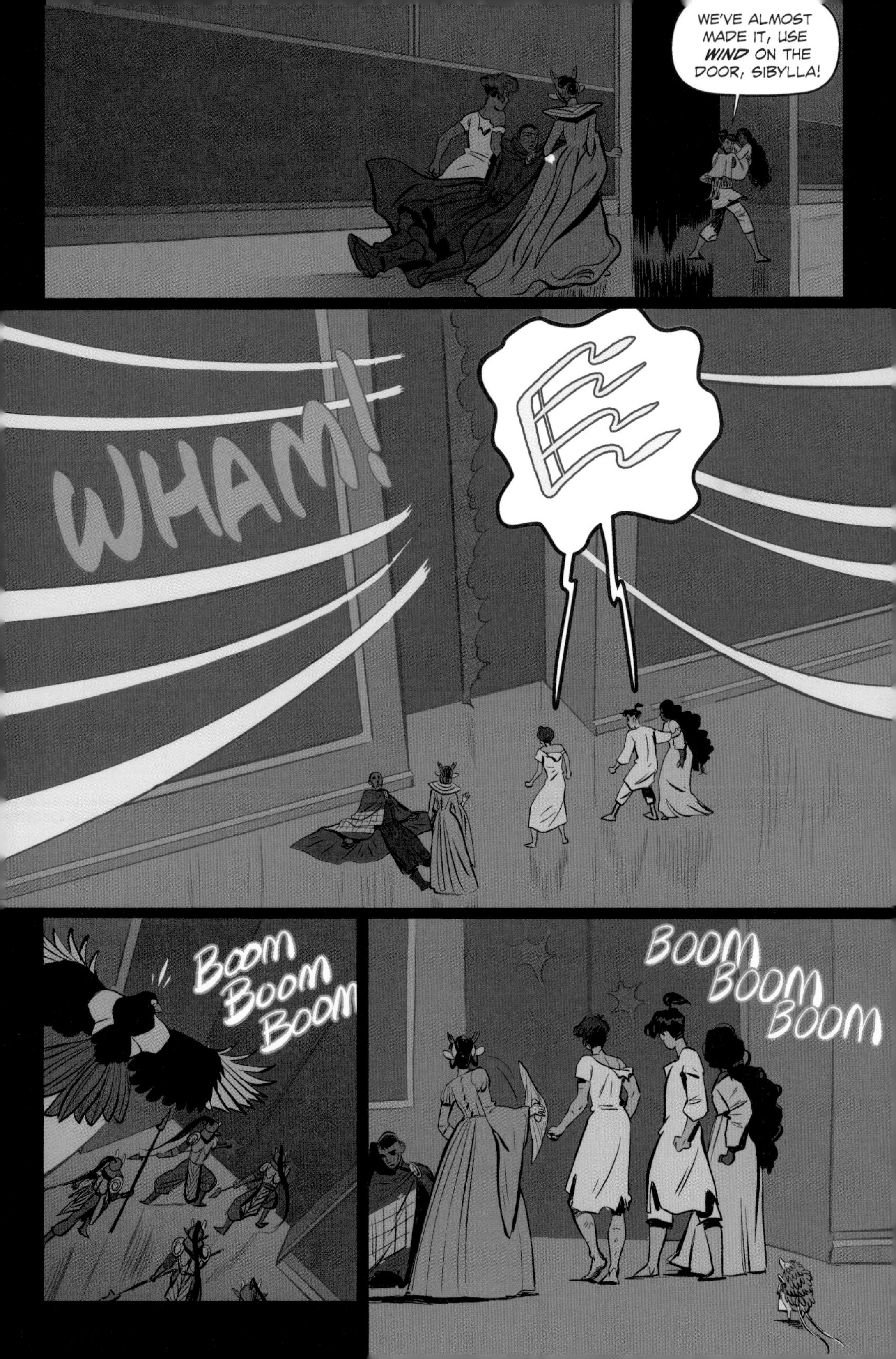
WE'VE ALMOST MADE IT, USE WIND ON THE DOOR, SIBYLLA!
WHAM!
Boom Boom Boom
BOOM BOOM BOOM

M-MISS—
WHAT?
MOPP, I'VE MADE A TERRIBLE MISTAKE.
I—OH, OH NO, MOPP. SHE'LL NEVER FORGIVE ME.
BOOM!! BOOM!! BOOM!!
I'LL SEE TO IT, JUST AS I ALWAYS HAVE.
COME WITH ME, ALL OF YOU!

EVERYONE! OVER THE WALL!

THE STREAM! DON'T–
WHERE...?
THE WITCH'S WOOD DOES AS IT PLEASES.

NO, NO, NO, NO, NO!
YOU DID A VERY BRAVE THING, PRINCESS. THANK YOU.
NO! THIS ISN'T WHAT I WANTED! I DIDN'T DO THIS FOR YOU!
I HAVE TO GET BACK!
YOU CAN'T, MISS.
BUT I DIDN'T WANT—
WE'VE GOT TO KEEP MOVING.
THERE'S A WITCH WHO RULES THESE WOODS, IT'S BEST TO AVOID HER NOTICE IF WE CAN.

THE WITCH'S WOOD.

AAAAA-
THUMP!
grackle

MAGGIE P!
PETRA!
MAGGIE P?
PETRA?
SO YOU'VE BEEN WITH BROM ALL THIS TIME?

WE FOUND HER WITH BROM... MAGZ-
IT'S PETRA. WHAT SORT OF A NAME IS-
I REALLY DON'T NEED TO HEAR YOUR OPINION ON THE MATTER.
grackle
LOOKS LIKE THE BIRD HAS AN IDEA.
GOOD FOR HER.

Pff-

LOOKS LIKE WE ARE... HERE...

MAIRE?

MAIRE? ARE YOU THERE?
WELL MET, SIBYLLA. PLEASE, ENTER.

A FEW HOURS LATER...
I AM SURPRISED HE STILL LIVES. YOU SAY YOUR MOTHER TOOK HIS MEMORIES?
SHE DID.
THAT WAS WISE OF HER.
THEY WEREN'T HERS TO TAKE–
NO. BUT THE CURSE WOULD HAVE FED ON THEM AND CHANGED HIM INTO SOMETHING... ELSE. THIS HAS SPARED HIM THAT FATE.
IT'S THE CURSE, IS IT? THEN THIS, ALL OF THIS, IS ON YOU.
IS THAT WHAT YOU THINK?

THAT'S WHAT I KNOW!
YOU WANTED TO PUNISH HIM, BUT NOW YOU'VE PUNISHED EVERYONE.
NORROWAY BROUGHT THIS DOWN ON ITSELF.
NOT JUST THEM, MAIRE! DO YOU FEEL NOTHING?
WILL YOU TAKE NO RESPONSIBILITY FOR WHAT YOU'VE DONE?
THIS CURSE OF YOURS, YOU SENT ME ON A FOOL'S QUEST TO LIFT IT!
I WAS JUST A LITTLE GIRL, MAIRE!
A LITTLE GIRL WHO CAME TO ME CRAVING ADVENTURE. I ONLY GAVE YOU WHAT YOU ASKED FOR.
YOU REALLY THINK THIS IS WHAT I ASKED FOR? YOU THRUST THIS DESTINY UPON ME BECAUSE, WHY?
BECAUSE A LITTLE GIRL ASKED YOU IF SHE MIGHT SAIL A SHIP?
OR WAS IT BECAUSE YOU COULDN'T CLEAN UP YOUR OWN MESS?

PERHAPS IT WAS UNFAIR OF ME TO INVOLVE YOU, SIBYLLA, BUT I HAVE HOPE YOU MAY YET CHANGE THE COURSE OF THE CURSE.
I WANT NOTHING TO DO WITH YOUR CURSE! I WANT TO FIND GILLY, AND I WANT TO BE DONE WITH THIS– AND WITH YOU!
WHAT'S GOING ON?
IT'S HER! SHE'S THE OLD ONE. SHE STARTED ALL OF THIS.
SIBYLLA, WE ARE ALL OF US MORE BOUND TO THIS THAN YOU CAN IMAGINE.
IF YOU WISH TO FIND GILLY AND LIVE YOUR DAYS IN PEACE, YOU WILL SEE THIS THROUGH.
IS THAT A THREAT?
IT IS A WARNING.
KEEP YOUR WARNINGS. I'M DONE HERE.

AAAAAAAA

DO YOU REMEMBER WHAT I TAUGHT YOU OF HERB LORE? WILL YOU HELP ME TO EASE HIS SUFFERING?

IT WILL BE THE LAST THING I DO FOR YOU.

MOPP, ISN'T IT? FETCH ME THAT BOOK.

Y-YES, OF COURSE.

ROSEMARY AND SPRIG OF THYME, LOTUS BLOSSOM, DEADFALL PINE, MOSS THAT GROWS BENEATH A STONE, BLESSED THISTLE BLOOMED FROM BONE, GLADIOLUS, HYACINTH, FORGET-ME-NOT, AND SUMMER MINT...
I'M NEVER GOING TO REMEMBER ALL OF THAT.
I'VE A GOOD MEMORY.
YOU'RE COMING?
I SUPPOSE I AM.

ROSEMARY AND SPRIG OF THYME
MOSS THAT GROWS BENEATH A STONE
FORGET-ME-NOT
GLADIOLUS
HYACINTH
DEADFALL PINE
LOTUS BLOSSOM

THANK YOU... LOTA...
I DON'T WANT TO TALK.
JUST LISTEN, THEN. BROM WAS–
I ESPECIALLY DON'T WANT TO TALK ABOUT BROM.
I DON'T KNOW HIM AS YOU KNOW HIM, BUT I KNEW HIM AS HE WAS BEFORE AND–
HE WASN'T A GOOD MAN.
I TOLD YOU I DON'T–
PLEASE JUST LET ME FINISH.
WHY DO YOU HAVE TO SAY ANYTHING AT ALL?
BECAUSE I WANT YOU TO UNDERSTAND IT ISN'T JUST YOU WHO'S BEEN LED AROUND LIKE A FOOL!
I WAS A CHILD WHEN I WAS DRAGGED INTO THIS, AND I THOUGHT IT MEANT I WOULD GET TO BE DIFFERENT!
I WOULDN'T HAVE TO DO THINGS LIKE TEND SHEEP, OR A HUSBAND. I'D GET TO USE THE MAGIC MAIRE TAUGHT ME, AND GO ON ADVENTURES, AND BECOME A GREAT KNIGHT MYSELF.
THEN BROM ARRIVED AND TREATED ME LIKE A USELESS ACCESSORY...
A FEW DAYS INTO OUR JOURNEY, THERE WAS AN ARCHER. HE FIRED ON US AND–
BROM DIDN'T–
HE JUST RUSHED AFTER HIM.
I SAW...
IT DOESN'T MATTER.

I THOUGHT I WOULD FIND A GRAND ADVENTURE, BUT WHAT I FOUND WAS–
IT WASN'T HATRED. IT WASN'T CRUELTY... JUST APATHY. EMPTINESS. THE MOST MERCILESS KNIGHT IN ALL THE LAND, THAT'S WHAT ALL THE STORIES SAY. EVERYTHING I HOPED FOR–
STOP IT! OK? I ALREADY FEEL BAD ENOUGH FOR LOVING–
I GUESS WE BOTH HAD CHILDISH DREAMS, THEN. AT LEAST YOU HAD AN EXCUSE.
I WAS WORRYING ABOUT THE WEDDING, ABOUT WHETHER OR NOT HE TRULY LOVED ME BACK.
THINKING I WOULD BE THE ONE TO BREAK THE CURSE.
I DIDN'T MEAN TO MAKE YOU FEEL–
BAD? HA! WHAT AN APOLOGY. I ASKED YOU TO STOP AND YOU KEPT PRESSING ON.
FINE, YOU WANT TO TALK? LET'S TALK, SIBYLLA.
LET'S TALK ABOUT TRYING YOUR HARDEST TO PLEASE EVERYONE, BUT IN THE END YOU'RE MISERABLE AND NO ONE IS HAPPY!
IN FACT, THEY'RE UNHAPPIER THAN THEY'VE EVER BEEN BEFORE!
LOTA–
I'M TALKING NOW!
I LOVED HIM! AND I KNOW IT ISN'T ***ALL*** YOUR FAULT, BUT I'M SO ANGRY, AND I'M SCARED, AND I HATE YOU FOR WHAT YOU'VE DONE!

I DIDN'T MEAN FOR ANY OF THIS TO HAPPEN. I JUST WANT TO GET BACK TO GILLY. BUT KNOWING THE TRUTH-
DAMN THE TRUTH, SIBYLLA! DO YOU HAVE ANY IDEA- FORGET IT.
JUST... LET ME GRIEVE THE MAN I THOUGHT I KNEW, THE ONE WHO NEVER EXISTED.
YOU KNEW HIM FOR SEVEN YEARS. IT COULD BE...
MAYBE YOU KNEW HIM THE WAY HE SHOULD HAVE BEEN, WITHOUT THE INFLUENCE OF HIS FATHER.
AS IF THAT FORGIVES HIS HISTORY?
NO. BUT IT ISN'T YOUR DUTY TO PUNISH HIM, OR YOURSELF.

IS EVERYONE LIKE THIS? HIDING A THISTLE AT THEIR CORE?
I HOPE NOT...
WHY DO I FEEL SO GUILTY? WHY DO I WANT TO LOVE HIM STILL? WHY DO I FEEL LIKE I HAVE THE RIGHT TO FORGIVE HIM?
SOMETIMES GOOD PEOPLE DO BAD THINGS, AND BAD PEOPLE DO GOOD THINGS.
AND WHICH IS HE?
OW!
I DON'T KNOW. I HOPE THERE'S GOODNESS THERE, THAT IT CAN GROW AND HE CAN CHANGE.
MAYBE THAT'S WHAT THE CURSE IS ABOUT?
SEEMS TRITE. WHAT BRAMBLED HEART BECOMES A ROSE?

HAVE YOU FOUND ALL I ASKED OF YOU?
ALL YOURS.
hmph.

WILL HE BE ALL RIGHT?
I CANNOT KNOW THAT. THIS PROBLEM LIES WITH THE CURSE.
DOESN'T THAT MEAN IT'S YOUR PROBLEM, THEN?
I HAVE TOLD YOU BEFORE, SIBYLLA, THE CURSE HAS FAR OUTGROWN ME.
I COULD NOT HAVE ANTICIPATED WHAT IT WOULD BECOME...
IT FEEDS ON EMOTION—
ON GUILT, ON FEAR, ON REGRET.
THAT IS WHY BROM AND ESBEN HAVE SUFFERED ITS EFFECTS SO DEEPLY.
THEY TOOK IT INSIDE OF THEMSELVES.
AND NORROWAY ITSELF?
COMMITTED CRIMES WORTH THE REGRET.

MY FATHER... MY WEDDING WAS MEANT TO SECURE AN ALLIANCE BETWEEN NORROWAY AND THE TROLL KINGDOM.

WHEN I KILLED THE PRINCE AND FLED... THE BROKEN ALLIANCE, THE WAR THAT FOLLOWED... THE FEAR PUSHED HIM OVER THE EDGE.

HE SOUGHT ANYTHING THAT MIGHT PROTECT THE KINGDOM, AND WHAT HE DISCOVERED WAS OLD MAGIC.

A MAGIC OLDER THAN ***SPEAKING.*** A MAGIC OF ***SHAPING,*** AND ***BREAKING.*** THE VERY SAME MAGIC THAT BUILT THE GLASS.

HE WOULD HAVE DONE ANYTHING TO HAVE IT.

NOT JUST HER. HE STARTED WITH THE CHILDREN IN THE CHANGELING GROVE, THEN MOVED ON TO THE SONS AND DAUGHTERS OF THE GENTRY.

YOUR PEOPLE LET HIM SACRIFICE THEIR CHILDREN?

ONLY THE COURT KNEW...
AND BY THE TIME IT CAME TO THAT, THE NOBLES WERE IN TOO DEEP.
IT STARTED SO SMALL THAT EVERY CHOICE HE MADE FELT LIKE THE NEXT LOGICAL STEP.
THE SACRIFICES BROUGHT POWER, BUT THEY DESTROYED HIM. AND IN THE END, THEY DESTROYED OUR KINGDOM AS WELL.
THE FAMILIES OF NORROWAY FELT THEY DESERVED THE RETRIBUTION, AND IT WAS SO.
THEY CALLED ON ME TO CREATE THE CHAINS BY WHICH THEY HAVE SHACKLED THEMSELVES.
THE CURSE IS A SIMPLE THING. IT PERPETUATES ITSELF AND FEEDS ON MISERY.
THERE IS SOMETHING ELSE... THERE IS ONE FINAL BROTHER WHO STAYED BENEATH THE GLASS WHEN THE REST OF US HAD GONE.
I USED TO RECEIVE LETTERS FROM HIM, ONES I KNOW HE MUST HAVE PAID DEARLY TO SEND. HIS FINAL LETTER...
HE DESCRIBED DISAPPEARANCES, MADNESS...
I BELIEVE THE NATURE OF WHAT LIES BENEATH THE HILL HAS CHANGED.
I OVERHEARD MY MOTHER, AND MAL...
THEY'VE BEEN SENDING SOLDIERS INTO NORROWAY.

WHAT?
I DON'T KNOW FOR HOW LONG, BUT THEY'VE BEEN LOOKING FOR SOMETHING...
IT SOUNDED AS THOUGH THE SOLDIERS WERE VANISHING.
IF THE CURSE HAS FOUND A NEW SOURCE TO FEED ON...
WHAT ARE YOU SAYING?
IT'S SPREADING, ISN'T IT?
HOW MANY PEOPLE MUST SUFFER FOR THIS, MAIRE?
NORROWAY? THE TROLL KINGDOM? GOOSE VALLEY, EVEN? HOW FAR CAN IT GO?
IF IT PLEASES YOU TO BLAME ME, SIBYLLA, I CANNOT STOP YOU.
YOU HAVE HEARD THE TRUTH OF THE CURSE AND WHAT IT IS.

HOW CAN SOMETHING LIKE THIS EVEN BE STOPPED? IT'S NOT AN OBJECT THAT CAN BE DESTROYED, IT-
IT HAS A ROOT.
COUGH
COUGH
COUGH
COUGH
COUGH
COUGH

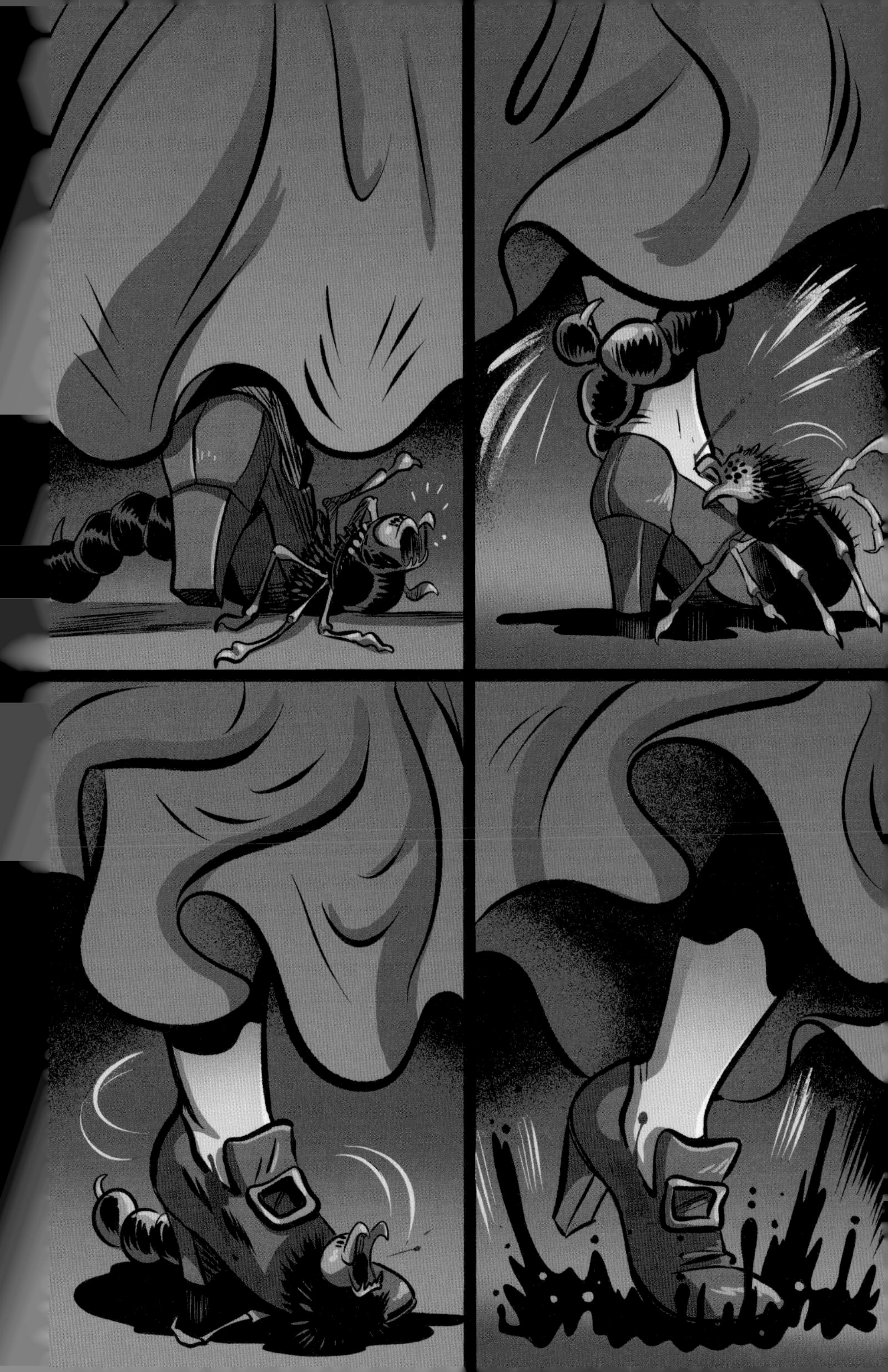

SIGH....
YOU MUST RETURN TO THE SOURCE, AND DESTROY IT.

WHAT... WAS THAT?
HE CARRIES THE CURSE WITHIN HIM.
IT WILL GROW BACK, I COULD NOT GET IT ALL, BUT I HAVE GRANTED HIM SOME TIME.
...WE NEED TO GO BACK...
GO BACK...?
TO THE PALACE! TO MY MOTHER! IF SHE UNDERSTOOD WHAT WAS TRULY AT STAKE–
ABSOLUTELY NOT.
SHE'LL HELP US. SHE CARES FOR HER PEOPLE! SHE WOULD NEVER WANT–
YOU'RE A FOOL!
YOU DON'T KNOW HER.
I KNOW SHE NEARLY HAD ALL OF US KILLED!

AS PUNISHMENT FOR CRIMES COMMITTED! OR WILL YOU DENY YOU RAN OFF WITH HER BROTHER'S WIFE?
YOU KNOW NOTHING OF WHAT YOU SPEAK-
ENOUGH.
WAP!
WAP!
LOTA FERNBORN, HARPER DHOW. YOU WILL NOT FIGHT WHILE YOU ARE UNDER MY ROOF.
COUGH

...I JUST THINK THAT IF SHE KNEW WHAT WAS HAPPENING, SHE WOULD HELP US TO STOP IT.
AND IF SHE ALREADY KNOWS?
SHE DOESN'T KNOW.
IT'S DANGEROUS TO RETURN. EVEN FOR YOU, LOTA.
SHE'S RIGHT, MISS...
I DON'T THINK IT'S A GOOD IDEA.

DAWN...
YOU DIDN'T STOP HER!?
SHE WANTED TO GO.
AND IF I WANTED TO JUMP FROM THE TOP OF THE GLASS, WOULD YOU LET ME?
I NO LONGER MEDDLE IN THE AFFAIRS OF MORTALS.
I– WHAT–!?
WHAT'S GOING ON?

MAIRE LET LOTA LEAVE!
GOOD RIDDANCE.
NO ONE'S GOING TO GO AFTER HER?
SHE HAS THE RIGHT TO HER OWN CHOICES, SIBYLLA. AS YOU DO.
BUT SHE'S MAKING A BAD CHOICE!
THEN WHY DON'T YOU GO AFTER HER?

LOTA!
WHAT ARE YOU DOING HERE?
YOU CAN'T GO BACK, LOTA.
SHE HAS TO KNOW!
WHAT IF SHE'S NOT THE PERSON YOU BELIEVE SHE IS, LOTA? WHAT THEN?
IF YOU KNEW HER YOU WOULDN'T SAY THAT.
EVERYTHING SHE'S DONE HAS LED ME TO BELIEVE OTHERWISE.
WHEN I WAS A CHILD... OUR VILLAGE WAS ON THE BORDER OF NORROWAY AND THE TROLL KINGDOM.
WE HAD NO DISPUTE AND YET... IN THE MIDDLE OF THE NIGHT, NORROWAY... THEY CAME AND THEY- THEY BURNED EVERYTHING.
I RAN INTO THE FOREST.
I WAS COVERED IN- IN BURNS AND ASH AND, AND SOMEHOW I ENDED UP HERE, OF ALL PLACES...

SCREAMING AND BLOODY AND HOWLING, I RAN TOWARD THE PALACE.
AND NOG TOOK ME IN. SHE RAISED ME AS HER OWN.
SHE'S MY MOTHER, SIBYLLA, AND I LOVE HER.
SHE'S... SHE'S GOOD. SHE'LL HELP US FIX THIS.
LOTA-

LOTA!

LOTA–
WHAT DO YOU MEAN YOU CAN'T FIND THEM?
WE'VE SENT SOLDIERS ACROSS THE STREAM, MY QUEEN. EACH OF THEM ENDS UP IN A DIFFERENT PLACE. IT'S THE WITCH'S MAGIC–
I DON'T CARE IF IT'S THE OLD ONE YOU'RE UP AGAINST! FIND THEM!
AND WHAT WILL YOU DO ONCE YOU'VE FOUND THEM?
I'LL KILL ALL OF THEM.
AND LOTA WITH THEM?
NO, NO. OF COURSE NOT. I'LL LOCK HER IN THE DUNGEONS UNTIL SHE LEARNS SOME SENSE.

MY QUEEN!
MOTHER, PLEASE!
DO YOU THINK I WANT TO HEAR WHAT YOU HAVE TO SAY?
WHAT YOU'VE DONE, LOTA–
MOM, I KNOW ABOUT THE SOLDIERS! I KNOW THEY'VE BEEN DISAPPEARING AND I THINK I KNOW WHY!

AND WHAT NEW PLAYER HAS BEEN FEEDING YOU STORIES?
ANOTHER HUMAN GIRL, PERHAPS?
THE WITCH OF THE WOOD. SHE'S THE OLD ONE. YOU HAVE TO BELIEVE ME–
BARE HER NECK.

MOM, PLEASE! THE CURSE IS SPREADING, IT'S...
SHE SAID IT MIGHT BE FEEDING ON THE SOLDIERS! IF IT COMES TO THE KINGDOM–
I THINK YOU HAVE SHOWN ME JUST HOW MUCH YOU CARE FOR THE KINGDOM.
PLEASE! HELP US! WE HAVE TO END THE CURSE BEFORE–
"WE," IS IT? AND WHAT "WE" IS THIS? THAT WRETCHED GIRL? THE CREATURE THAT BEHEADED YOUR UNCLE AS HE SLEPT? A FOREST WITCH? DO YOU THINK THESE PEOPLE CARE A WHIT FOR THE KINGDOM, LOTA?
WHAT DO YOU THINK WILL HAPPEN IF THE CURSE IS LIFTED? IF THE KING IS FREED? DO YOU HONESTLY BELIEVE THIS PEACE THAT WE HAVE FOUGHT FOR, THAT WE HAVE BLED FOR, THAT WE HAVE DIED FOR WILL LAST?
I SHOULD HAVE SENT TWO ARCHERS TO KILL YOU, I SHOULD HAVE SLAUGHTERED THAT BULL WHEN I HAD THE CHANCE.
I WON'T MAKE THAT MISTAKE AGAIN.

THUMP!
SWOOP!
SWOOSH
WAP!
MAGZ!

LOTA!

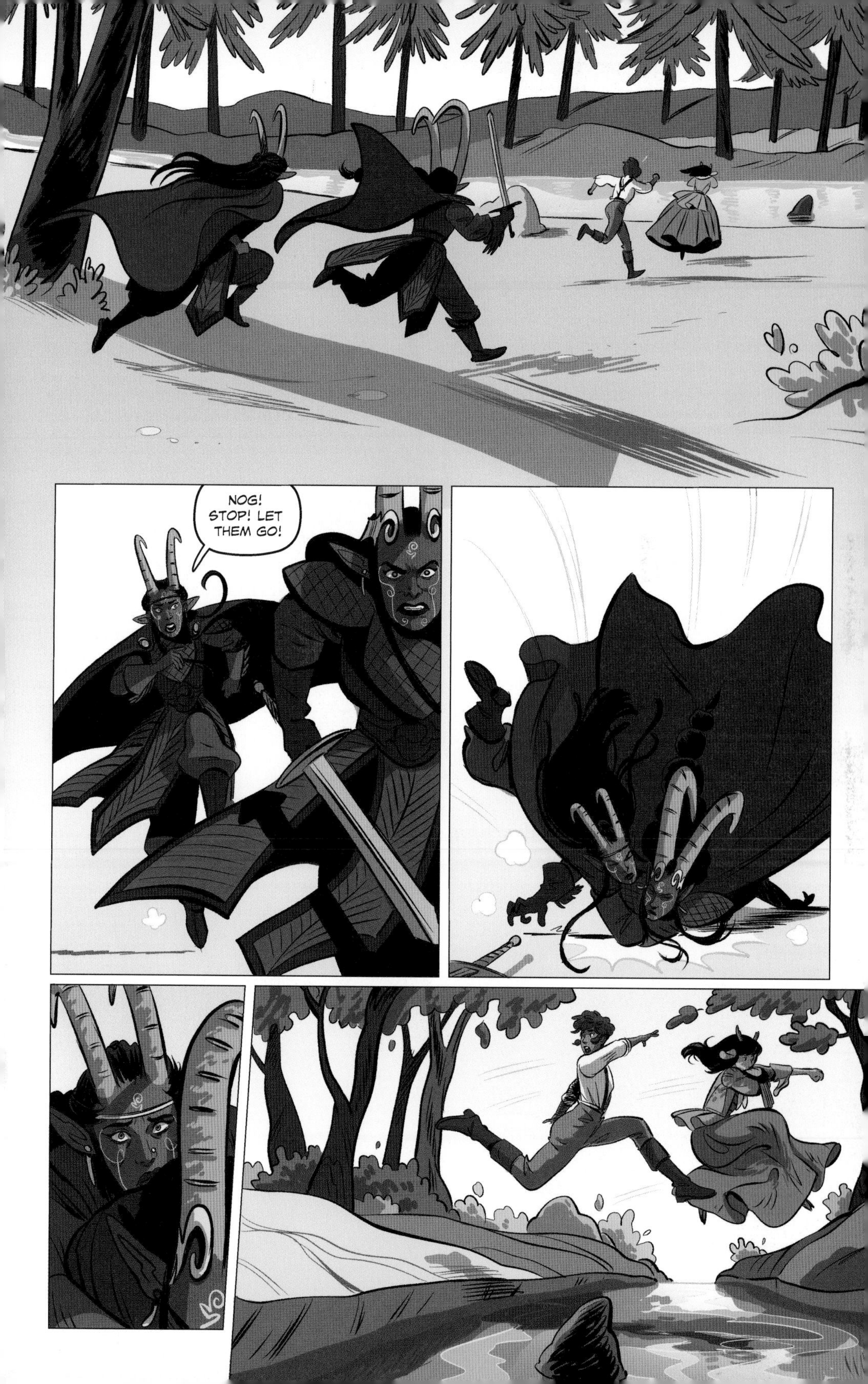
NOG! STOP! LET THEM GO!

IS SHE-?

WHIMPER...

I REALLY THOUGHT SHE WOULD LISTEN TO ME...
I DIDN'T.

I DON'T– I THOUGHT I KNEW HER. I REALLY THOUGHT...
AND THEN I COME TO FIND OUT I DON'T KNOW HER AT ALL. I THOUGHT SHE WAS TRYING TO BRING PEACE TO THE TWO KINGDOMS WITH THE WEDDING, WITH THE UNIFICATION. BUT I HAVE NO IDEA WHAT SHE WANTS!
WHY SHE SAVES WHO SHE SAVES, WHY SHE HURTS WHO SHE HURTS... ASSASSINATIONS, THE SOLDIERS...
I'M SORRY, LOTA.
DON'T BE.
I'M COMING WITH YOU TO NORROWAY.
I BARELY KNOW THAT I WANT TO GO!
YOU HAVE TO. NOTHING IS SAFE NOW.
NOT THE TROLL KINGDOM, NOT YOUR GILLY, WHEREVER SHE MIGHT BE. MY MOTHER...
I HAVE TO KNOW WHAT SHE'S BEEN TRYING TO FIND, WHAT SHE WANTS FROM THAT PLACE. IF THERE'S SOME-THING THERE THAT'S CHANGED HER–
THEN IT'S SOMETHING THAT COULD CHANGE US TOO. LOOK AT WHAT'S ALREADY HAPPENED TO PETRA.
PETRA SAVED US! AND...THAT'S WORTH THE RISK OF WHAT WILL HAPPEN IF NO ONE–
I DON'T WANT THIS RESPONSIBILITY.
WHY DO YOU ACT LIKE YOU'RE THE ONLY ONE WHO GETS TO CHOOSE!?
IF YOU'D NEVER COME INTO MY LIFE, I WOULD BE HAPPY AND AT HOME. YOU DON'T GET TO CLAIM THAT YOU HAVE NO FAULT! YOU DON'T GET TO RUN AWAY!
AND IF YOU DO, THEN YOU HAD BEST CONDEMN YOURSELF RIGHT ALONG WITH MAIRE, BECAUSE YOU'RE NO BETTER.

I-

YOU'LL NEED TO GO BACK THROUGH GOOSE VALLEY IN ORDER TO GET TO NORROWAY.
THE EDGE OF MY FOREST IN THE TROLL KINGDOM IS TOO CLOSELY GUARDED.

ONCE YOU REACH THE NARROW SEA, YOU SHOULD TAKE *THE FLEETFOOT.*
...ABOUT *THE FLEETFOOT.* SHE–
CRASHED INTO A BUNCH OF ROCKS WHEN DHOW TRIED TO KILL BROM AND ME.
STILL HOLDING A GRUDGE, ARE WE?
ESBEN MAY BE ABLE TO HELP US.
THEN GO TO HIM.

...YOU'RE NOT COMING?
OH, NO, MISS. I'M STAYING ON TO HELP MISS MAIRE.
MOPP IS VERY TALENTED.

THANK YOU FOR EVERYTHING, MOPP. I'LL SEE YOU AGAIN, ALL RIGHT?
OF COURSE, PRINCESS. I'LL LOOK FORWARD TO IT.

BE BRAVE, ALL OF YOU.
YOU HAVE MANY TRIALS TO COME.

EARLY NORROWAY SKETCHES...

SIBYLLA

LOTA
MOP
NOG
MAL
GILLY
EDUN
RHADA
EDIE

FLORENCE BEA

LOTA

oxboxer.tumblr.com | jsalume@gmail.com

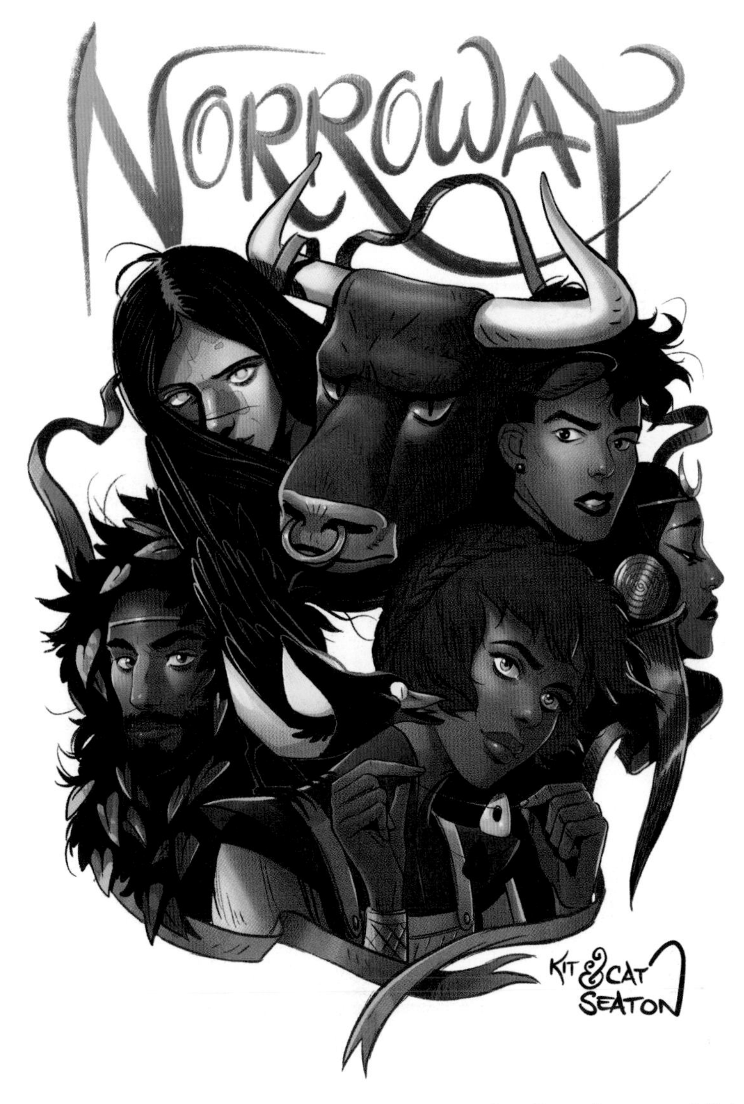

No book is made without the help of friends, family, editors, publicists, printers, readers, and all the other lovely folks who flit in and out of our lives. Whether you've been with us from the beginning or you've just arrived, we have only gratitude and love for you.

Thank you to everyone who has had a hand in this. Thanks to our parents, Nils, Maleia, and Michelle, and our friends, Leila, Kendra, and Briah. A special thank you to Lisa Brennan. And finally, an especially special thank you to our heroic, our legendary, our spectacular editor Shanna, who put up with so much to make this book possible. This is your baby as much as ours.

Thank you, readers, thank you, fellow comic creators, and thank you, Image—for everything.

Thanks!
—CAT

ALSO FEATURING
LISA BRENNAN
THE ADVENTURES OF
FISHBOY AND ONIKID
FIND OUT MORE AT
WWW.FISHBOYANDONIKID.COM